ROMAN ANIMAL TRAPPER

Also by Mayo Purnell

BESTIARIUS

Roman Animal Trapper

by Mayo Purnell

I

It started in Baalbek, in the Lebanon, where Lucullus Turbo happened to be when the Caspian region was cut off by the recent uprising in Mesopotamia. In a hotel room overlooking the precinct walls of the massive sanctuary of Jupiter Heliopolitanus, he'd been en route to Hatra, a Roman client principality four hundred miles east on the Silk Road, where the legionary garrison was to lend him support on a trapping expedition in the tiger-rich forestlands bordering the Caspian Sea. The problem was, that garrison wasn't there anymore, just fly-buzzed carcasses rotting across the rocky terrain with the black-smoke remnants of their camp drifting lazily into the sky. And so there was Moas, that viperous piece of shit, who was getting more expensive every time.

Turbo and the Syrian merchant were old adversaries, but the animal trapper had several hundred thousand sesterces of his own money tied up in his project to bring tigers to Rome for breeding purposes. A job of some difficulty, since the species didn't do well in captivity, and mating them under such circumstances proved even more difficult. But Lucullus didn't like to be thwarted once he'd set out to do something. His Latin mind sought the ordering of his experience, and the exclusion from it as far as possible of the incomprehensible, the disruptive or adventitious.

He glanced through the window at the temple a stone's throw away. Built of the superb, honey-gray local limestone, his hotel room was on a level ten feet below the fifty-foot podium atop which its seventy-foot columns thundered in silence across the rectangle of his window. His eyes ran across the finely-wrought baroque montage of the temple's entablature and cornice. Its pedimented gable wavered a hundred feet above him, surmounted by a sculpture group of Jupiter driving a chariot of colossal bronze horses. He squinted, and turned his mind back to the present reversal of his fortunes.

The courier from the city magistrate's office had left his room not an hour before, a young boy, polite, in a white tunic. He bore a scroll and a severe manner learned from his elders, and his explanation made painful sense. The Persian vassal states had overthrown their Parthian overlords and made a quick and successful try for Hatra as a message to Rome. Bypassing Baghdad, Ctesiphon and the old token capital of Babylon, it was more a symbolic statement than a strategic one, severing Asiatic trade for a moment, a luxury artery to the heart of the West. Turbo tipped the courier and dismissed him with a request for the hotelier to bring up wine, and he stood in grim silence as the boy's footsteps faded hollowly on the tiles.

The sun had begun its descent, and the tremendous Temple of Jupiter was jagged with the raking shadows cast by its geometric forms and sculptural decor. Beyond it the less-large but still-huge Temple of Bacchus towered above the colonnaded portico of the far precinct wall. Unlike the rose and blue smoke of a sunset in Rome, which misted the pines and opened his senses to the adventure of the night, sunsets in the East had always struck a disquieting note in Turbo's soul, evoking a sense of the futility of human endeavor and the meaninglessness of life. His business, his pleasures, his fears and ambitions, were revealed as no more than dust and broken toys by its molten glow. He glanced at the courier's scroll and his face grew worn, his eyes old. And then they fell upon the clay krater of wine.

He shifted his muscular legs over the bedside, rose and walked to the low wooden table against the wall where the Arab boy had left the tray with its krater and cup and a small bowl of figs. Pouring the cup to the brim, he quaffed it in one gulp. Again he filled and emptied the cup, and then again. When he set it down, a fine warmth stole through his veins. Things and happenings assumed new values. The Syrian sunset faded into others when life was good and real and vibrant after all, not the punishment of a jealous god. He filled another cup, walked to the window and stared at the bloody orb, conscious of himself and his task, its magnitude and import. The star was no stranger to him, for his father had been a Legatus in the XVth Legion Apollinaris, and Lucullus grew up under the standard of the sun god.

Born in Rome, Turbo's parents had moved with him to Egypt shortly thereafter when his father was posted to command a cohort of the Apollinaris in charge of the Claudianus Mons, near the shithole of Gebel Fatireh, where the larger share of the granite adorning Rome came from. Three hundred and fifty miles down the Nile near the coast of the Red Sea, a prehistoric landscape of wadis, deep gulleys, ancient ravines and eroded mountains, the Emperor Claudius had claimed the property as a quarry a century and a half before, and thus its name. Under Trajan it became a penal colony for extracting the massive monolithic columns that were more and more to become an indispensable signifer of the grandeur of Rome.

Augustus boasted that he had found her a city of brick, and left her a city of marble. In any event, throughout the early empire, the metropolis began taking the perfection of Greek forms and changing the materials with which those forms were construed. In time, the Italian peninsula was no longer enough to satisfy the corrupt desires of wealthy Romans for greater and wilder color patterns, and neither was its current slave market enough to extract them. As the Empire grew and expanded, more and different kinds of marble natural to certain areas in the world became available, as did more slaves; and the capital added new colors accordingly. Whole ships were specially built to bear the weight of the massive blocks, and Rome's enemies, misfits, criminals and undesirables – those not lucky enough to die in the Games – were sentenced to dig them out of the earth.

Quarries dotted the hundreds of miles of desert between the Nile and the Red Sea – the Ophyates Mons for the green granites, Aswan for the reds; the Porphyrites Mons for the purple and black porphyries, Hammamat for the green breccia. But from the Claudianus Mons came the lion's share of the columnar granite, the so-called 'Granite of the Forums' – serene gray and speckled with quartz – also the rare marble known as serpentina, mottled like the skin of a snake, and precious to the Ancient Egyptians.

Thus Lucullus' childhood was spent under the whine of levers and pulleys, the groan of cogwheels, the crack of whips, and the screaming sound of the lathes on which the massive columns were spun smooth while teams of oxen, elephants and mules marched in circles driving the tremendous mechanical systems that motivated them. Symphonic accompaniment to his boyhood play, their ungodly cacophony was regularly punctuated by the earth-splitting sound of fissuring cliff faces and the insane moaning of vast blocks of granite as they fell onto mountainous cushions of cut palm trees. The boy would jump and leap, and frolic among the thousands of columns that lay about in half-finished states of work, or climb with his friends – the castaway sons of other Roman officers – on the mountain of potsherds from the broken amphorae used by the Arab lackeys to transport water to the prisoners from the closest well two miles distant.

Yet, on certain days, he strayed away from the ungodly screaming of the lathes, the inhuman cracking of the whips, and spent the hours among noontime silences on wavering plains vast enough to absorb all constructive thought patterns. Each evening for the boy was an actual participation in the sunset, and he remembers the desert at night, tribal fires flaring against the wind. In the mist of the evenings, part fog, part dust from the cattle returning to the kraals, to milking and sleep, the ridgelines looked like worm-eaten faces screaming in silence, and he and his friends often escaped to abandoned caves and explored by torchlight the tombs of exiled gods.

Tremendous wood beams, rotten scaffolding, splintered wedges and the gigantic iron spikes used to create fault lines in the cliff faces – these were Lucullus' childhood toys. His favorite was an experimental column that weighed two hundred tons. Nicknamed the 'mother of all columns,' it had lain near the huge ramp of mud and stones which brought it down from the cliff where it was extracted over a hundred years before, and then proved too heavy to transport. For the columns had to be drug one hundred and twenty miles through the Wadis of

El Markh and Hammamat to the Nile, where they were loaded onto vast barges that displaced their weight.

The barges were often helped along by teams of elephants pulling on huge chains from the river bank, as the granite shafts were floated and rowed the three hundred and fifty miles downriver to the port of Alexandria. There they were registered by the particular corporation officiating over their sale, and then loaded onto the Naves Lapidariae, the 'stone ships' specially constructed to bear their weight and transport them the twenty odd days across the Mediterranean Sea to Ostia, the port of Rome. At Ostia, they were again registered at the particular corporation's offices in the Forum of the Corporations, before making their way up the Tiber to form another piece of the Eternal City.

Twenty and thirty-foot monoliths were common sizes; and even the forty-footers, which weighed sixty tons a piece, such as those of the great Pantheon's portico. A fifty-foot monolith was the largest possible in terms of smoothing, transporting, and erecting, however; for the ten extra feet actually doubled the girth from that of a forty-footer to come in at around one hundred and twenty tons. The Temple of the Divine Trajan in Rome had a porch of twenty-six such columns, all quarried from the Claudianus Mons.

But the two hundred-ton 'mother' wasn't going anywhere. And when young Lucullus reached an age in life where he could climb atop her, trot down her length, and throw his fellow playmates off to fall ten feet into dust-puff impacts in the sand below, he thought there was nothing left on earth to conquer. But then came the years when athletic conquests weren't enough, and there were other forms of conquering which he came to desire. In the Wadi, the penal colony where the granite workers went home to their cramped quarters to celebrate the day's end with a pittance of bread and water, he would wander the streets at night under the stern gaze of the legionary guards with the dim suspicion that life was passing him by.

Though the town had the classic configuration of a Roman provincial city – the decumanus with its flanking and cross streets bisecting the pitiful little wattle and daub huts – there was nothing but hundreds of miles of misery in any direction. Two streets led out from the gates – one in the direction of the quarries, the other toward the small hill overlooking the city where the contingent of legionaries and their commandant, his father, guarded the concentration camp. Higher up was the pitiful little Capitolium, which, like those of all provincial Roman cities took its cue from the Capitoline Hill in Rome. It had its temple to the Capitoline triad of Jupiter, Juno and Minerva and, inside the sanctuary, the base of a weathered statue of Trajan in typically rough, provincial craftsmanship announced that 'Annius Lucullus Turbo of the XVth Legion Apollinaris at the time of the Emperor Septimius Severus was in command of the marble works at the Claudianus Mons.'

After ten years there, and despite yearly trips to Alexandria, his parents began to show signs of depression. Though his father was a relatively humane commandant, it wasn't an overly uplifting atmosphere being around fiends sentenced to digging their own graves every day. Lucullus was fond of his parents, and it hurt him that his mother sat and stared, and his father lost himself in a haze of alcohol and soft middle age, wondering at how life had stranded him with men stationed to their deaths east of Hell and west of Eden, doomed to drink wine watered with their own falling sweat in the perpetual slave-stink of skin cancer and leprosy – one sunburned, scroungy unit of force preserving the emperor and the granite of Rome against any threat east of the Red Sea.

As a consequence, and despite their infinite efforts – the project to start a proper school for the camp children, the Greek tutors hired from Alexandria (none of whom lasted more than a few months) – Lucullus grew as wild as the desert surrounding him on every side. When he wasn't trapped by the tutors, he used to follow the engineers from Rome around like a surly dog – tough contractors whose world consisted of mathematics, stone and whores; he learned from their hardness. Or he placed bets with his friends on his ability to lift and throw bigger and heavier chunks of granite, or tear down young palm trees with his bare hands. But, in time, none of it was enough anymore; and he began to yearn to break out of the familiarity of his surroundings as all young men worth their salt do.

Needless to say, sex was catch-as-catch-can at the Claudianus Mons, and you didn't turn much down. Lucullus took what he could get like the rest of them – old beat-up whores from the camp brothel who'd give him freebees, the rare treat of a friend's sister – the only thing he ever turned down was a smooth-skinned little Arab boy who carried water for the prisoners. And he turned him face-down. But mainly he just spent his teenage years horny, mad with the itching of lice and heat rash, and well familiar with the exquisite torture of masturbating back the boredom under these conditions.

The first time he ran away his father tried to whip him, but Lucullus quickly subdued the sad man while his mother screamed and tore her hair in the background (it wasn't the life she had imagined for herself). Lucullus burst into tears and slid down the wall and then went and hugged his father on the floor and his father hugged him back and he began to ride the Nile on the barges which transported the columns, pavement disks and marble veneer to Alexandria. His parents allowed him to do so, for they knew he was stifling and that he was rapidly reaching an age where he would do it regardless.

On the Nile the boy came into contact with the sailors, mercenaries, roving intellectuals and stateless philosophers who plied their lonely trades throughout the Empire, and he fell under the spell of these men who didn't fit in, whose home was wherever they happened to lay their heads. According to Aristippus of Cyrene, the wise man is a stranger everywhere, and Lucullus garnered an education from these types, and learned from them how to pick his battles and play his advantages. Their schooling came easy to him, for he was by nature saturnine and intelligent.

No one can overcome the impressions of earliest childhood, and the boy's brain developed in a world of massive mechanical systems, of physics and mathematics, engineering and slavery. But later it was these loners, and, above all, one other impression that planted a seed in his thirsty soul. For one day on that great artery that led to and from the heart of the dark continent, the boy gazed across the water from the cache of dragon columns he rode to a barge loaded with something much different. Cages containing beasts, and men not much less wild than the cargo they traded in, Lucullus never forgot his first sight of the fly-covered lions panting and staring at him through the bars, the tribal spearmen sullen and staring as well, melancholy and painted with mud so dry that it had become white on their muscled black bodies, giving them a look as of demons from the underworld. And it was then that his heart began to stray farther away from the whine of the levers and pulleys, the groan of the cogwheels, the cracking of the whips and the ungodly screaming of the granite lathes, toward the screaming of the wilds of nature. It was then that the attraction began, the pull of the places where the gods went to revel in their darker saturnalias.

After his sight of the lions on the river, something had changed; and his father began to allow him to take place in the traditional legionary hunts, a practice that supplemented their recreation and kept the men somewhat militarily sharp. The kill of a desert leopard in an Egyptian gulley was his first taste of blood and courage, of danger and split-decision. And he found a release in the confrontation between human intelligence and the instinctual wisdom of the beast which, through the years, would turn into a medium for God.

But when he killed a legionary in a fight over a young prostitute from the camp brothel whose sadly beautiful, faintly oriental eyes had taught him everything he would ever know of love, his parents thought it a good time for Lucullus to leave the Claudianus Mons. And so they enrolled him in the Mouseion, the elite university system at Alexandria which had grown out of the famous library; and sent him there the usual way – on a barge with a load of columns bound for Rome.

City of the Ptolemaic kings founded by Alexander the Great, ferment of culture in the Mediterranean Basin, a flower of Greece in the dead garden of Egypt, Alexandria was the most cosmopolitan city in the world. And though Rome had ruled her since Augustus' defeat of

Antony and Cleopatra two hundred years before, her Greek intellectual legacy had lived on. The sense of any given place was always strong with the boy; he'd ridden the river past Memphis time and again, climbed the Great Pyramids at Heliopolis, seen Thebes with his parents and scratched his name on the base of the Colossus of Memnon. At Alexandria he lived in an atmosphere which had bred some of the most ground-breaking theories and discoveries known to man – water pumps, steam engines, the diameter of the Earth and the heliocentric hypothesis. And he walked in the footsteps of some of the biggest names in the history of the human intellect – men like Archimedes and Euclid, Eratosthenes and Aristarchus of Samos. At the library which had become a university, and which was founded by Demetrius Phalerus, a follower of Aristotle, there wasn't a manuscript anywhere in the world that wasn't available; and the apt pupil mastered Greek, studied philosophy, and developed a grudging love for poetry. But it was while riding the barges back and forth between visits to his parents that his brain began to understand the commerce of Empire, to deconstruct it into need and fulfillment. For Lucullus was Roman to the core.

As his father was a high-ranking officer, he was privy to the social elitism of the expatriate Roman community at Alexandria. And though he detested the fashionable liberalism of their dilettante society, his natural intelligence acquired a veneer of polish which more and more hid the wildness beneath it. Yet as much as it was hidden, it festered within him all the more; and it combined with a natural streak of independence and a desire to strike out on his own and create a reality and a fortune for himself which grew with his budding intellect and his knowledge of the scope and potential of the world he lived in.

During these years while Lucullus was at university, the Empire began to undergo the upheaval which was to characterize it for his entire adult life. And it was one last impression that sealed his fate, as he sat reading poetry on the docks of Alexandria one fine autumn day. For two weeks the Mob had been rioting uncontrolled in the streets of Rome. The economy of the greatest Empire in the world was unraveling like a worn-out tapestry. The cost of maintaining Rome's vast war machine, the latest catapults, ballistae and fast war galleys, was draining the commonwealth dry, not to mention the constant subsidies that had to continue to be paid to the satellite nations dependent on her for support to keep them from revolting. The government was bankrupt and couldn't stop the riots in the capital.

The young student was squatting with his back against a tremendous obelisk from the reign of Tutankhamen, which Caligula had ordered transported all the way from Thebes to Alexandria before being assassinated. As a consequence, the project of bringing it to Rome had been abandoned, and it had lain on the docks for a century and a half. Covered with hieroglyphs, Lucullus had found a spot in its shade where his back fit comfortably into a huge ankh and was reading Ovid. It was a beautiful day, sylvan clouds trailing across the vast indigo blue of a Mediterranean autumn sky. The white-stucco houses, shops and bazaars of Alexandria spread across the arc of the bay and the huge lighthouse loomed one hundred and fifty meters over the lesser towers and temples, the bronze statue of Poseidon atop it sparkling in the sunlight.

A commotion on the docks caught his attention. And, as he listened, he realized he was watching an argument of some consequence. For the Port Legatus was pleading with a captain of the Imperial Shipping Fleet.

'The merchant fleet is awaiting loading,' the man had said, obviously a young patrician who still had ideals. 'The ships can be loaded with either grain for the Mob or with the special sand used on the track for the chariot races. Which shall it be?'

'You fucking twit,' the captain had screamed, though the Legatus outranked him. 'The situation's out of control. The Emperor's insane, the eastern Legions are mutinying and the Mob's out of food. By Mithras, load the sand! We have to get their minds off their troubles!'

Lucullus smiled as he imagined the publicity campaign that would be pushed throughout the capital, thousands of sign painters attacking its walls with venue announcements, heralds sprinting through the streets and standing on the lips of the grand fountains in the squares of Rome announcing that the finest chariot races on record would be held at the Circus Maximus. As intermission features, hundreds of gladiators would fight to the death and thousands of condemned criminals would be torn apart by wild animals. Fights between elephants and rhinos, buffalo and tigers, leopards and wild boars would be staged for betting purposes and, as a special feature, twenty Nordic girls would be raped by baboons. Admission to the rear seats, free. Small charge for the first thirty-six tiers...

As a solitary, unused to speaking of what he saw and felt, Lucullus had mental experiences which were both more intense and less articulate than those of a well-adjusted man. They were sluggish and wayward, and never without a melancholy tinge. At university, sights and impressions which his colleagues passed with a glance, a light comment, a smile, occupied him more than their due; they sunk silently in, they took on meaning, they became emotion, adventure, vision.

For the young man of poetic bent, dissatisfied with the web of weaknesses, impositions, dubieties and half measures involved in the normal business of living, the scene on the docks at Alexandria was one such impression. He closed the passage of Ovid, which moved him no less. But, as with his first sight of the fly-covered lions sliding by, panting and staring at him through the bars of their cages with the green river sunlight sparkling murder in their eyes, something opened inside of him, briefly, frighteningly, as if a small window flung onto a vast, dark, dreadfully beautiful plain. And the resonance within him increased.

The limits of his allotted field, of what he could hope for, had long seemed dissatisfactory to him – a position of minor import in the affairs of Roman Alexandria, perhaps even a teaching position at the Mouseion, for his professors found him talented; in any event a life of mediocrity, of civil servitude. But when he saw certain scenes that gave him inspiration, when he had certain visions like those given him by a dusk of Virgil, then those limitations became blurred and he broke through them at certain points. The sight of lions and the gigantic commercial machinery of the Empire were such visions. And when he experienced them, life became a cyclopean, wild-eyed, ebony-skinned negress who lay moaning before him with her thighs spread wide. And Lucullus' soul moved, grinning horridly, toward the dark crevice between.

II

After staying up much of the night pouring over his leather parchment maps, the next morning Turbo saddled up and set out on horseback with his team of Nubian spearmen overland to Palmyra, city of palms – fortunate possessor of an abundant water supply and a consistent political connection with Rome since Augustus stabilized rule in Syria two centuries before. They made the hundred odd miles along the watering holes in two days, coming from the south upon the city's outerlying rows of lush palms late in the afternoon of the second, when the great disk of the sunset rode the silhouette of the massive Temple of Bel, its crowstep merlons etched like sharpened teeth against the smoldering orb.

The corridors of palms which gave the city her name yielded to her famous colonnaded thoroughfares as they entered one of the many triple arches stationed along the way toward the interior. Situated in the heart of the Syrian desert at the crossroads of east-west trade, Lucullus well knew that Palmyra's meteoric career as a merchant city was due to the setting up and policing of a system of regular caravan routes, which offered the merchants engaged in the fabulously rich luxury commerce between Asia and the Roman World a safe and direct outlet to the ports of Palestine. Her architecture was Imperial Roman with a strange, almost Indian accent; precursor of dreams and the late, fanciful, Hellenistic style which the great Alexander's wars spread throughout Persia and Mesopotamia. The columns of her colonnades bore statues on brackets halfway up their shafts, a tidy solution to the clutter of civic statuary at ground level with which most Greco-Roman cities were content. The long stretches were thrown in phalanxes of shadow across the thoroughfare as Lucullus and his crew clopped wearily down it seeking lodgings for the night.

The trapper cut a strange figure when he traveled outside of Africa, followed as he was by a train of sullen, six-foot blacks who didn't talk much. The Nubians were extremely loyal to him, however, and would do whatever he asked, even dig up corpses in village cemeteries to feed the beasts they'd captured on their way to the coast in a pinch. They'd seen him kill a leopard with a knife once, and they held him to be different, special; perhaps even a minor, fallible god. When he was drunk and dangerous around campfires at night, their blood-shot white eyes stared at him in silence through the wavering glow, their nostrils quivering at his passage. The smell of his spirit in such moments left them somber and uncomfortable.

After establishing his men in a cluster of rooms above a tavern that had a stable, Lucullus set out for the temple district with the night-time desert coolness lifting the dusty smell of the sandstone street slabs. The evening echoed with the shouts of tavern mongers, the laughter of children, the clatter of carts, and the whispered solicitations of prostitutes who eyed his fine form as he passed. The smells of cooking, of cumin and Indian curry, gave him a pang of nostalgia for the East; a sense of deep mystery and great antiquity which he enjoyed, but never felt comfortable with. He always felt the need to watch his back there, take a corner chair in the taverns if he could get one. Not like the lush pine and fir forests of Middle Europa, where a friend was a friend and an enemy an enemy; and where the black bucks hopped through the misty mountain forests.

Bordering the eastern perimeter walls of the Sanctuary of Bel, the streets became badly lit and dangerous. On all sides of him the temples shone in the moonlight, sandstone pillars and bronze domes and silver arches, shrines of the East's myriad strange gods, their rituals intricate and complex, their essence lost in a maze of formulas and rituals. Viperous eyes watched him behind bead-curtained doorways that filtered a seedy orange light and the dank smell of hashish. He turned down several side streets to arrive at the forecourt of Moas' townhouse.

Lucullus had organized several expeditions through the merchant with the objective of re-establishing the trade connections that had been languishing since the Parthian Wars under the Severans closed the Tigris and

Euphrates routes. But that was fifteen years ago and he hadn't seen Moas in a while, aside from a few transport squabbles over Caspian game, for the Arab also had offices in Sidon, Tyre, and Caesarea. Major ports for Mediterranean traffic, Moas dealt in whatever you wanted – Indian spices, Chinese jade, drugs, silk, animals, little girls, boys, and anything in between.

"Welcome indeed, my dear friend! How good it is to see you!" exclaimed the corpulent Arab merchant in a swirl of robes, sticky fingers and fleshy lips which slobbered their kisses on each of Lucullus' cheeks.

"Cut the bullshit, Moas," the trapper replied, grimacing at the greeting. He knew the fat queer would just as soon have him knifed in an alley than look at him. He also knew that he knew that he needed a favor which would elicit rich compensation. Otherwise he wouldn't be there.

Half an hour later he lay propped on his elbow on a reclining bench of red silk upholstery with dull brass legs, glowering around the rough, blocky, vaulted Eastern architecture and holding out a silver goblet to receive the rich ruby wine which the jewesses waiting on him moved about with, their delicate flittering slippers rasping across the coarse slabs of veined Assyrian sandstone. Oil lamps dangled from bronze chains in the vaults, their light bathing him in a deep orange glow. One of his slimly-muscled legs hung off the couch, and a blood-gorged vein ran down the meat of his calf into his sandal. He

21

wore a red tunic of double-stitched quality, open at the neck to reveal his corded throat, trapezius and collarbones. With his short-cropped blond hair combed forward in the classical Roman manner, his high brow, slightly snubbed nose, cleft chin and the watchful blue eyes that had squinted through thirty-six summers, the trapper was a fine example of the more fairly-complected Latin race that grew up on the hills around the Tiber. As opposed to the darker Italic types which they soon-after subjugated.

He slowly rolled the goblet of wine between his fingers – surprisingly articulate, their skin cracked like aged leather – his hands livid with scars from the years of pulling and grabbing and working with things that bit and tore without remorse. He took a sip of his wine and touched his mouth with the back of his hand, his striated forearm flaring back from the leather band that gave support to his wrist when handling boar spears or antelope horns.

"If I can get down the Euphrates to Charax," he said, "I can hit the Persian Gulf and coast hop to Barygaza, the main northeastern Indian port." He lifted an olive from its silver platter on the low dining table. "We've still got connections with the Raj down there, and I know a tiger-rich pocket about a hundred miles inland. I'll trap cats, and procure rhino, elephants, and whatever else I can afford from the Raj," he explained, chewing pensively around the pit of the olive, "and send them up the overland caravan routes with your people."

"Ah, my noble Lucullus," Moas raised a jeweled paw, "if there is one thing that I admire about you Romans, it is your fantastic sense of the possible," he said. "Of the possibility of overcoming obstacles, of surmounting them." The merchant inserted a candied date through his sausage lips before he went on. "This is what makes you such brilliant builders of bridges and highways, such great engineers."

"Cut the bullshit, Moas," the trapper replied, the pit of his olive between his teeth. He swallowed it. His grandmother had believed they were good for the stomach.

The merchant raised his hand again, humored as always by the behavior of his time-honored acquaintance. "I, however, come from a much older culture," he said. "We know our limitations. And the limitations of the world we inhabit."

Lucullus sighed, tired as always at having to weather these half-assed political discussions which inevitably came back around to how Rome was forcing itself upon the world unwantedly. He poured himself another goblet of wine. "I didn't come here to discuss sociology."

"To get down and get the job done," Moas continued, settling to business, "will take you . . ." he counted on his jeweled fingers, "three months."

"Right," replied the trapper, scooping a spoonful of goat cheese from its pristine silver bowl. "That will make it winter, and in time to catch the monsoon," he said, spreading the cheese across a piece of the thin crisp Syrian bread that lay stacked to the side. It was now the month of Thoth, he reflected, of September. "It's up to you to get the bigger game back up the caravan routes."

The monsoon blew from the southwest in summer and then reversed and came back down from the northeast in the winter. If you misjudged it you ended up like one of the skeleton ships that mariners making the crossing in the early days sometimes came upon. After drifting in the doldrums rowing in circles for a thousand miles, their crews finally just gave up and lay down on the deck and died and rotted into salt-parched skeletons grinning at empty horizons. But Lucullus had made the crossing more times than he could count, and when you hit it just right with that wind at your back, it only took two weeks to cross the thousand nautical miles of the Arabian Sea to the Spice Cape of East Africa, where he knew a good whorehouse he could stretch his leg in while the animals were stretching theirs in the retaining pens.

He just hadn't counted on having to switch to the Indian market this late in the game, and having to get down the Euphrates to do it, which would be tricky, since everything east of the Tigris had recently been destabilized; so the tiger-rich regions of Persia weren't options anymore. India was still a viable option, but Moas was the only one who had the connections necessary to get him the five hundred miles down the Euphrates to the port of Charax on the Persian Gulf. But, more importantly, Moas was the only one who had the connections to get the big game back up the caravan routes. You could only take so many elephants and rhino across the Arabian Sea. The opium didn't work so well on the big creatures, and when an elephant went mad in the middle of the ocean, you had a real problem on your hands. And when three or four of them went mad, you drowned.

"Ahhh but times are hard, my friend," the Arab trader assured him in a swell of black robes and a huff of adjusting his girth on the dining couch, obviously irritated that times were indeed hard. "As you're well aware, the Sassanian Persians have recently overthrown the Parthian monarchy, and are currently laying siege to Ctesiphon and Baghdad."

"I know," nodded Lucullus, in a mock display of patience. "That's why I'm here."

"And the lawless raiders," the merchant continued unfazed, "who always take advantage of these interim situations," sucking date off its pit, "are harrowing my barges below Seleucia," he smacked his lips. "Scandalous."

Lucullus knew the nomadic Iranian horse-archers only too well. He had lost twenty-three men and a caravan of animals to them during the last period when Rome and Parthia were under an uneasy truce and he'd sent an expedition out of Alexandria to trap game in southern Persia. He grimaced. The garden of civilization had always been a hotbed for the

Greco-Roman world. Five thousand years of culture – Sumerians, Babylonians, Assyrians and Hittites – assimilated into the Persians, who made a try for the whole of Europe until the Greeks stopped them. Then Europe made its try for the East, the Great Alexander driving all the way to the Himalayas and marrying his generals to the daughters of all the satraps along the way. But then the Greeks petered out and the Parthians rose up out of the plains of central Asia east of the Caspian Sea and drove all the way to the coast of Palestine.

The Romans didn't really know they had a problem until twenty thousand of them were killed at Carrhae by the shock of Parthia's heavy cavalry and the rain of death from their archers. Now a re-juvenated Persian empire had sprung up out of a line of vassal kings, the Sassanids, who were formerly subject to Parthia. And in each of these power vacuums, the Arabs, like Moas, picked up the commercial pieces and scavenged the losers. Like they did the Romans that escaped the disaster of Carrhae, hunting them down in desert gulleys and killing them for their armor and belongings, whatever they could sell in the scrap bazaars at Antioch.

The corpulent merchant popped another candied date through his fleshy lips and shook his head sadly. "And, my noble Lucullus, the mercenaries I use to protect my business are getting more expensive every year."

Lucullus stared at the carved reliefs circumventing the silver platter on which the jewesses had left the gold-embossed, green glass carafe of wine. Greek craftsmanship with Homeric heroes and bacchanalic scenes of orgiastic gods, the faces of those aloof Olympians seemed to be laughing at him now, as they dealt their capricious blows of fate and fortune in no more than party games. Well, they had dealt him Moas now. Of course Lucullus did not believe in the gods. But, all the same, he was bankrupt if he couldn't deliver the goods.

Animal trapping was a tough, thankless business. And without a deep interest in the beasts, and a personal fascination with their habits, it was better left alone. But Turbo possessed the above qualifications. And his life had more than once been determined by possessing them.

He saw himself as a charter member of an austere fraternity going back much longer than the hundred and fifty years the Colosseum had been around, but the numbers and variety of animals being used had gotten progressively more freakish as time went by. Titus had five thousand wild beasts and four thousand domestic animals killed during the hundred days of shows he threw to open the great Amphitheater in Rome. Forty years later, Trajan gave a set that lasted a hundred and twenty-two days to celebrate his Dacian Triumph. Eleven thousand humans and ten thousand animals were killed.

The logistics of acquiring the beasts wasn't appreciated by the Mob in Rome, but it was the bread-and-butter of Lucullus' livelihood. By this point in his career he'd seen whole provinces cleared of animals to satisfy the demands. Most of the Nile hippos were gone, and the African and Indian rhinos were in danger. The European lion was almost extinct, the aurochs, the Libyan elephant and most of the remaining African bears. The collecting and shipping of these animals was an enormous industry. An industry which, if the games were to be abolished – as Marcus Aurelius would have liked – would threaten to collapse the Roman economy. For whole provincial cities were dependent upon it for their livelihood, and wild animals were the most valuable gift a barbarian monarch could make to his Roman overlords.

Lucullus had been to what is now Norway for moose and elk. He'd been to India for rhinos, cobra and elephants; and deep into the heart of Africa for everything else. He'd trapped lions in Mauretania, boar in the Black Forest, and bears as far as the Baltic.

Organizing these hunts was a tremendous undertaking. As was to be for his foiled Caspian expedition, the Legions were often pressed into service on the drives – a supplement to both their training and recreational activities – and he'd worked with the Italica and the Claudia in what is now Bulgaria, as well as the Danube fleet out of lower Moesia. He'd drafted entire village populations by Senatorial Authority for the work, crippling their local economies for weeks. But the hard part was not so much getting the animals as shipping them. Taken by ox cart to the nearest coastline, or floated down rivers on rafts, the journeys could take months, and keeping the animals alive, not to mention himself, could become an ordeal.

This was where the great merchant conglomerates came in, who used bribes, blackmail, murder and just plain money to get the beasts through zones at war and at peace. They complemented the columns with mercenary escorts, and established way stations along the caravan routes where the animals could be released into large enclosures for periods of rest and exercise. Local villages were often required to provide food for the animals, often under threat of force, whether by the mercenary escorts or a contingent of legionaries.

And then the journey by ship to Ostia was also a long and tenuous affair, especially the Red Sea route from India, which was a difficult sail by any means, what with its treacherous reefs and shoals, and the fact that the voyages often had to be made at night to spare the animals the heat of the sun. Opone and the Capo Gurardafui were the main African ports for the Indian routes, and all galleys stopped there to be loaded with rice, sesame oil, ivory and other animals bound for Italy. Local tribes were pressed into forced labor, hauling cages, loading and unloading cargo, their fields often stripped to feed the beasts – just one more example of the overweening truth that a human life meant nothing in comparison to the needs and appetites of the Urbs that has become the Orbs, the City that had become the Universe. Needs which required an immense amount of blood that had to be spilled in sacrifice to somewhat capricious and oft-angered gods. For the games were still thrown under the auspices of a religious ceremony, and the Romans loved animals.

The trapper took a long draught from his jeweled goblet and kept the wine on his tongue for a time. He swallowed and let his breath hiss out in a sigh between his teeth. The wine was depressingly excellent. "How much, Moas?"

"Ahhh, my friend . . . but now we're truly speaking," the merchant raised a carefully trimmed and colored eyebrow. "And aren't things so much more pleasant when you don't shout?"

III

Dura-Europos spread before Turbo like an ugly whore after a long dry spell. They crested a rise and there she was, sunburnt and miserable under a cratered moon hung gray the color of aged meat in the purple-blue sky. The Euphrates slid by her side like a lazy green serpent, and he and his crew started down the rise toward its back, the sunlight heliographing off the spear tips and sword pommels of their mercenary escort. After three days spent riding in silence with the suspicious Syrian mercenaries and his sullen Nubians through cracked white alkali and low ridgelines you never seemed to reach but only pass, and two nights spent sleeping around campfires kept burning to frighten the jackals away, he was almost glad to see her.

Sandy white figures atop the rock and mud-brick walls shouted and waved their arms as they approached, figures in voluminous robes such as the Sand People wore, their heads wrapped in heaps of rags against the unforgiving sun. A strange greeting; as Lucullus got closer, he realized that these faintly disturbing figures were Roman legionaries, and their antics no greeting at all, but rather a warning to steer their horses clear of the caltrops and butterfly clips scattered across the terrain under a light coating of sand. The sharp steel spikes were cripplingly effective against horse and camel hooves and Dura – the former Greek city of Europos – was expecting a Sassanid attack at any time.

Founded five hundred years before in the wake of Alexander the Great's campaigns, and settled with tremendously unlucky colonists from Macedon; on the breakup of the Seleucid Empire three hundred years before – a kingdom of Mesopotamian satrapies that stemmed from Alexander's general, Seleucus – the town passed into the hands of the Parthians. Except for a brief interlude when Trajan drove the Roman eagles to the Persian Gulf a hundred and twenty years before, Dura had remained in their hands until seventy years ago, when it was again occupied by the sons of the she-wolf. Yet, despite the tarnished medallion with the rampant lion emblem of the XIIIth Legion Gemina hanging above the portal, when Lucullus and his motley crew of Nubians and Moas' mercenaries clopped their thirsty horses through its tired timber gates groaning inward on rusty hinges, it looked like the pendulum was about to swing again.

The camp commandant greeted them with a permanent tick at the corner of his mouth and a constant blinking of one of his eyes. The trapper noticed it, as did his Nubians, who smelled quirkiness like animals did. As their chief and he went through the usual white man's witch-doctor ceremony of greeting, the tribesmen shifted their dust-covered feet in the sand, calloused like flattened cauliflowers from the years of running behind Turbo's horse. They were duly established in a barracks along with Moas' Palmyrene mercenaries, whose captain was invited with Lucullus to bathe, and then dine, at the commandant's residence.

The emperor Septimius Severus had made Dura an important garrison installation after sacking Ctesiphon, the Parthian capital three hundred miles south on the Tigris, thirty years before. Nearly a quarter of the area within its rock and mud-brick walls had been expropriated for the building of barracks and officers' quarters, a headquarters building, a parade ground, several bath-buildings, a small amphitheater for the recreation of the troops, and an official residence for the commander of the Euphrates frontier zone – the Dux Ripae, or 'Duke of the River Banks' – as he was officially known.

The post was currently filled by the man with the tick and the blink, whom they followed on horseback, flanked by his two bodyguards – big, windburned, mean-looking mothers in the new style of banded cuirass, their matted black hair worn long and braided. The trapper guessed by their traditional felt caps that the bodyguards were hangovers from the special cohort of Spartan hoplites raised by Severus' son, Caracalla, for his own Parthian campaign fifteen years before, when the young emperor had fancied himself a new Alexander and set out to emulate his eastern wars. The five men clopped through the maze of narrow dirt alleyways past Dura's torturous, shop-fronted dwellings.

The houses were flat-roofed and mostly single-storied, with the rooms grouped irregularly around small courtyards in the local Mesopotamian manner. The temples, with their columnar porch-fronts, were as superficially Western in feature as the classical names given to the divinities worshipped within them. For though it had been an official Greco-Seleucid colony, Dura had rapidly taken its place within an older world in which local Semitic influences were strong enough to absorb and orientalize its original Macedonian settlers. As at Baalbek and Palmyra, the Romans studied attributes of the native gods and matched them with those of the traditional Western pantheon to facilitate peace and commerce. Yet the thin veneer of Greco-Roman religious syncretisms at Dura still couldn't cover the deep antiquity and darkness of what were essentially Babylonian agricultural deities. And their forms of worship had remained distinctly native.

The town's current inhabitants were a morose mix of locals, the wives and concubines of its garrison, and the military prostitutes, of course; a sad lot of baggage train irregularly rotated around the brothels attached to Roman installations in Syria. Lucullus saw the defeat in their young-old eyes as he passed a few trying half-heartedly to look appealing in the city center, which had long reverted from its Greek beginnings into a busy Oriental bazaar quarter.

In its Roman phase, a little order was established by the erection of streetside porticoes along the most important frontages and by the opening of a market square with shops grouped around it, where the trapper saw several hundred soldiers encamped under hastily established tents with a weathered statue of Apollo rising in oxidized bronze from their midst. Legionaries in subarmilii – linen tunics with small square pockets stuffed with woolen padding that acted as undergarments for the heavier battle armor – the men lay on their backs or played dice on pentagrams cut by their daggers into the pavement in the light green shadows beneath the stark white tarps in the saffron glare of the desert afternoon.

Lucullus remarked the random assortment of 'Vexilla,' or unit banners, rippling infrequently in a wind that was nothing but waves of heat. He knew that it had become increasingly rare for complete Legions to leave their provincial bases and take the field anymore. Since the last Parthian war, the tactical situation in the Empire had become such that detachments, or 'Vexillationes,' better served it in terms of speed and logistics. Acting as fire brigades, these small battle groups massed in appropriate numbers could tackle large armies or be dispersed to quell revolts. They also provided strong garrisons for towns, road junctions, passes and river crossings, such as Dura.

From the banners with their insignia and the various animal motifs on the neatly stacked cylindrical shields, Turbo noticed contingents of the XIIth Legion Fulminata, the VIth Ferrata from Syria, the Vth Macedonica, and what looked like an entire cohort of his father's old troop, the XVth Apollinaris from Palestine. He realized that the build-up he was witnessing was neither guard force nor garrison, though; the men were en route to Hatra with the objective of relieving it. Yet he also knew that their mother Legions in Syria and Palestine had already been depleted to support the Rhine and Danube regions, which were under incursive attack, thus severely reducing the effectiveness of any response in Mesopotamia.

The commandant's residence was finely situated on the low cliffs overlooking the river, and laid out in the Roman manner around two peristyle courtyards. On one of its wings was a small bath-building, where Lucullus and the Syrian mercenary disrobed, and entered the caldarium situated to catch the afternoon heat. The shallow dome of mud and fired-brick was displaced in the age-old Mesopotamian manner with the bricks pitched on edge across the line of the vault instead of being laid radially as in normal Roman work. It caught Lucullus' eye, for it was little things like this that told him he was no longer wholly within the frontiers of the Empire.

And yet travel had become as life to him. Though he had a spacious house in the center of Alexandria, and a nice flat in Rome, his real abode was the touch and smell of bare earth. His constitution had adapted accordingly, and he could subsist as well on British gruel or tainted German meat, on African beetles and the goats' blood of his Nubians, as he could on the succulent pork of Rome, and her smooth Falernian wine, which he also had a weakness for. There was a part of him in which it was all the same; in which it had to be the same.

That sameness was important. It was the sameness of Marcus Aurelius, of Epictetus and the Stoics. It was the sameness which he lived by, but did not wear on his sleeve.

From a young age Turbo had developed the intrinsic feeling of not wholly belonging to any one place save perhaps to Nature herself. A foreigner in every land, yet in no place did he feel a stranger. For he experienced the cold of Scythia, the rain and mud of Britannia, and the curious colors of dawn on the Black Sea, as if they sprung forth from his very Self. Which, of course, they did.

He and the Syrian sat in the hot room beneath the vault with its ragged little oculus, sweating and scraping the desert grunge from their bodies with styrils and sipping tepid water from terracotta gourds against the dehydration. As the trapper loosened and stretched his travel-stiffened limbs, the mercenary took in his frame out of the corner of his eyes. Though neither tall nor particularly large, Lucullus' knotted muscularity was woven in and out of a litheness of limbs which indicated the potential for both spring-coiled explosiveness and nimble agility. It was this, and the fact that some of his scars looked like they should have been killing wounds, that made the hardened captain of Palmyrene horse-mounted archers decide that, if he ever had to, it would be best to dispatch the trapper unknowingly to avoid severe and, perhaps, permanent physical damage.

After they had bathed, they dressed rather incongruously in the Chinese silk robes placed at their disposal by the servants, whom they then followed across the colonnaded courtyard through the paths flanking the rock-bordered garden plots planted with wilted oleander and dusty palms, the daylight in retreat across the desert sky above. The dark decor of trophies of war lined the back walls of the peristyles, Parthian standards and cataphract armor from Severus' campaigns thirty years ago, staged at intervals between medallions of the late emperor, watching from pools of darkened bronze shadow. Lucullus noticed that they hadn't updated the medallions. Perhaps they were on order.

Inside the dining room, the torch in its bracket on the wall was in competition with the pale liquid orange of the dying day streaming through the arches of the western porticoes. The strange halflight wavered like a mirage through the room where the commandant sat on a low-legged couch with his forearms across his knees, starting occasionally as a random shot from one of the ballistae mounted atop the flat rooftops of the palace, or the battlemounts around the town's squat walls, rang out across the river valley to the accompaniment of the faint, far-off, and rather unbalanced laughter of its crew. The artillery pieces resembled huge crossbows and shot bolts like gigantic steel javelins, their crews aiming for the millennial detritus of boulders and ancient shepherd's huts dotting the near ridgelines, gambling on hits over their evening allotment of wine.

"The Roman public thinks that Parthia is a conquered country," the commandant abruptly sputtered, gesturing sheepishly at the low table set with platters of olives, dates, hard cheese and dried meat; and then pouring wine for the two as Lucullus and the Syrian took seats.

"It is." He shook his head, blinking. "But not by us," he said. "Our last two wars with them destabilized them enough that the Persian revival which began fifty years ago is now complete," he tapped his finger on the low dining table. "So just be careful what you're dreaming," he smiled, ticking at the corner of his mouth. "For soon your dreams will be dreaming you." He grabbed up his old-fashioned Greek drinking bowl and took a hasty sip, shaking his head and placing his wrist to his mouth with an indigestive gesture of his chest.

"The high priest of Anahita in Persis married the daughter of a local satrap he'd dislodged in a coup d'etat and Artabanus, the king of Parthia, refused to recognize it," he continued. "Then the high priest's son, Ardashir, succeeded his father and declared himself king of Persia. Artabanus tried to get the king of Ahwaz,

39

another of his vassal states down there, to bring them to heel." He shook his head, "Ardashir crushed him and then marched on the Parthian army and defeated them in three successive battles. He hung Artabanus' head in the Temple of Anahita at Persopolis," he smiled and blinked and took another hasty drink from his bowl, "Not the fucking Parthians anymore," he gasped, pounding his fist into his chest and laughing as if something was really very funny, and as if he was about to cry.

Lucullus squinted his eyes at the man sitting there in his fringed white cloak clasped at the throat by the bronze eagle medallion and worn over a white tunic with the purple stripes indicative of his Senatorial rank. He took in his white leggings, and how they ended in rather dainty black slippers. And he had the strange and somewhat disquieting sensation that he was looking at Marcus Licinius Crassus, commander of the Roman forces at Carrhae two hundred and seventy years before.

Crassus, after recently crushing the Spartacus rebellion with armies he'd purchased through his banking successes, was riding high politically. And, like the commandant sitting before him, was representative of Rome's demand that her citizens of Senatorial or Equestrian rank take part in public affairs. During the initiation of a ten-year war between Rome and Parthia over control of Armenia, Crassus' son commanded the Gallic cavalry, the light troopers, the foot archers, and eight cohorts of the Legions.

In the initial engagement, the Parthians betook and decapitated the young man and paraded his head before the Roman lines on a spear. Then they offered his father his life if he would surrender, giving him the night to mourn the death of his son. During the night Crassus lost self-control, and it fell to his two subordinates to develop a plan to leave the wounded and retreat under cover of darkness.

Turbo finished his wine and refilled himself, admiring the Greek craftsmanship of the krater and drinking bowls – Macedonian, and original; they had somehow survived the five hundred years of rape and pillage Dura had seen, and were now in the shaky hands of what was very probably their last caretaker. He raised his bowl slightly, nodding at the commandant and the mercenary captain, then brought it to his lips for a long draw . . . Knidian, past its prime, bittersweet.

Another bolt from one of the ballistae hissed sickeningly out over the river, and Lucullus' eyes lifted to the porticoes and through them towards the crimson tide smoldering across the horizon. Somewhere over there was Rome. His world. And not his world.

Crassus' own head was used in a performance of Euripides at the palace of the king of Armenia, where the Parthian king was residing as a guest while he conducted the campaign. The actors tossed it from hand to hand

41

like a ball in the course of a performance of the 'Bacchantes;' an allegorical drama contrasting the barbaric military practices of Asia with Hellenic culture, which a barbarian king with a smattering of Greek learning had presented on the afternoon of a victory over Rome.

The trapper brought his mind back to the present.

"The garrison at Ctesiphon defected to Ardashir," the commandant was saying, with one eyebrow raised, his other eye blinking in time with the twitch at the corner of his mouth. "Two thousand men." Then he shrugged, as if to dismiss the matter. "The Parthian army wasn't much after we sacked and burned the place fifteen years ago. Only the second time in sixty years."

Lucullus caught a glimpse through two of the piers of the western portico as one of the long-abandoned shepherd's huts on the near ridgeline exploded in a slow-blossoming flower of dust and rocketing stone flecks which rose to illumination in the great bloody gas ruin of the sunset. The sound ricocheted off the hills, causing the commandant to jump, and then blink faster and mumble irritatedly. "Do you have a barge ready?" Lucullus asked. "If so, we can leave tomorrow."

"Barges," the man flicked his hand dismissively. "We have barges." He smiled angrily. "Ardashir won't be ready to come against us for a little while yet. He's busy trying to reunite the tribes spread over Persia and

Mesopotamia which the Parthian breakup disunited. We're trying just as fast as we can to buy them up but," he blinked and ticked and smiled with bitter irony, "not enough time . . . not enough money."

"It should take us a week to reach Babylon," the trapper continued. "Another to reach the Persian Gulf." He looked at the Syrian, whom he was starting to realize he might have to kill. Moas would be humored to no end, and besides, he had only given half of the money up front, the rest would be paid upon delivery of the big game to the port at Sidon.

"The bulk of the Persian forces are regrouping on the other side of the Tigris in Elymais and Media," answered the commandant, not seeming to have heard. "Their archers are the best in the business. They get them from the Saka and the Yue-Chi people," he blinked and twitched. "Their heavy cavalry alone could probably take any army that Alexander the Great ever put in the field." He refilled his bowl, spilling a bit on the sandstone inlay of the low bronze dining table. "They know the oases and their men can live on boiled leather for weeks," he said. "They've got a contingent up giving grief to Hatra, but that won't matter much either way. The real battles won't come until later," he smiled sadly, as if he wouldn't be there to see them.

"Can you give us any indication of what to expect on the river?" Lucullus asked patiently.

"What you're up against is a shattered Mesopotamia," the commandant replied. "Sand People, tribal warfare, rape, looting, lawlessness. It's chaos down there," he shrugged. And then he raised his voice in a surprisingly clear tone of command. "The map please, Julian!"

An adjutant presently entered from an antechamber, producing a scrolled map on vellum parchment which he unrolled on the low dining table and the men subsequently steadied with the krater and their wine bowls. A young patrician with a sculptor's model of tight dark curls, square jaw, a dimpled chin and a handsome Roman nose, the adjutant wore the white linen subarmilis with its grid of square padding, a ring-buckled belt with open-work plates, and the old-style dagger.

Lucullus perceived quality in him, for he liked his men with a future and his women with a past; and he took him in the way he did the fleeting enjoyment of a sip of fine wine as the young man traced a finger over the route, the gold signet ring indicative of his promotion to Equestrian rank glinting in the torchlight.

"You'll have to stay on the Euphrates," the youth said, "take the river fork south through Babylon. The city is mostly abandoned now, though there was a contingent of the Fourth Scythica holding out there," he looked up and paused, as if searching for the correct terminology. "We have no idea of their status," he concluded, shaking his head grimly. "I wouldn't stop there."

44

The trapper met the young Roman's eyes and then glanced at the mercenary captain, who sat silently all the while. He thought he detected a slight sneer on the man's face, though it was hard to tell with these types. In any event, he was starting to develop a real dislike for the man. For his false, arrogant eyes, his evident cruelty and his pretentious dress. But he needed him through Uruk, below Babylon, where Moas had a contact at the old Seleucid toll station who could supposedly negotiate with the tribes and, if need be, the Persian as well as the Parth, in terms of getting the big game back up. It was starting to look like things were going to get a whole lot worse before they got any better; and it was unwise to take a gamble on buying the big game if they weren't going to make it back. Which meant that he was going to lose most of his collateral.

In terms of staying on the Euphrates, Turbo assumed as much, for thus they would avoid the hotbed of Ctesiphon on the Tigris, where Ardashir had gained total control. And yet, as pointed out to them on the map by the adjutant, there would be a tight stretch in which they were no more than twenty-five miles from the city. Lucullus was neither surprised nor impressed by the fact that the capital's occupational garrison had defected to the Persian usurper. What could you expect of Armenian conscripts, raised since childhood to resent the Roman?

He and the mercenary captain reviewed river logistics with the adjutant while the commandant wrote correspondence to the unit commanders he would lead into the desert the next morning. The man had the smell of death about him; Lucullus had sensed it too many times not to recognize it. The trapper reckoned the relief of Hatra would be last post for him, but he dismissed the matter, and turned his mind to the task at hand.

Highway of trade and commerce for thousands of years, the Euphrates was a civilized river and, if their luck held, relatively smooth, without rapids or falls. Lucullus reckoned that the upheavals of the last half century wouldn't have been enough to allow it to grow wild again. Save the usual unforeseen circumstances he had grown accustomed to over the last half of his life spent trapping wild animals on the frontiers of the Empire.

They settled on a price for the barge, one big enough to handle his Nubians and the mercenaries, nineteen in all. Turbo subtracted their horses from the price. They'd get them killed before they got very far out of Dura. Their only hope was to trash the barge and disguise themselves as a poor colony of Sand People, preferably lepers. The commandant blinked and ticked and signed the deed with a stilus and then held a candle to two waxen seals and stamped it with the lion symbol of the XIIIth Legion Gemina, then the sunburst seal of the XVth Apollinaris.

The latter grated across the trapper's filial heart, as had the sight of its Vexilla in the market square. "I thought the Apollinaris was posted in Germania now," he mentioned in passing.

"The Apollinaris was raised in the East during the Parthian Wars under Nero, when they were harassing our efforts to solidify Armenia," responded the commandant. "It was transferred to the Danube five or six years later under Titus, after the sack of Jerusalem. Then it returned to the Orient thirty or so years later under Trajan." He nodded his head, blinking. "Since then it's predominantly been stationed at Carnuntum in the Alps, and in fact was the Legion I was first posted to. The Gemina is a branch-off," he explained. "But we're all a bit split-up," he smiled, ticking and blinking, "these days."

After the conference, the trapper walked out into the town's maze of narrow dirt and pebble alleyways, where he sought to shake off the tremulous commandant and the morose mercenary like lice from his brain in the quickest possible way. Several of his Nubians followed silently in his wake as he walked through a maze of phantom legionaries half-heartedly chasing whores through the streets, past the wavering torchlight of their more austere contingent dining in silence in the Mithraeum. He saw others still, gathered about hookahs in the dirt courtyard of the smallish precinct of the Temple of the Palmyrene gods built into an angle of the city walls. Not only positioned on the principle

47

Greco-Roman invasion route into Mesopotamia, but also at the crossroads of the famous 'Silk Road' between East and West, for which it acted as a customs point, Chinese opium and the resinous blossoms which grew all over Bythinia and Armenia were readily available at Dura.

He declined their offers to join them and got drunk instead, in a tavern with three nineteen-year old Italics from the verdant green of Campania high on sunburn, disillusion and the End. Pawns caught up in the Mesopotamian obsession with the Greco-Roman West, the boys spoke of their mothers and their milkcows, and Lucullus paid for the stringy lamb, the bowl of steamed greens and the loaf of stale bread. The young legionaries ate without talking, then thankfully left, and the trapper sat and drank in sullen silence, watching an Armenian dancer twist her oiled belly on a table to the seductive strains of an oboe played by her brother. An open coin purse on the floor with a few coppers in it told their story.

Later, back out in the street, the dancer's tickling had become an itch; though he didn't have the heart to buy her in front of her brother, no matter how many times it had been done before. Thus he ended in a heap in a cheap military whorehouse, while his Nubians stood silent guard at the door. And he wondered how it had all gone so wrong; and also how he'd developed such an itch in the shithole of Dura rather than in Palmyra, which had it all – Chinese teens or anything else one might fancy.

But though what he found had been rode hard, she helped him along with the stress a little, as a breath of stale air might a drowning man, running her long, cracked, old, twenty year-old fingernails over his chest and torso as he reached climax the only way he ever could – on his own.

He even spoke with her a bit afterwards, the least he could do. Like others of her kind she had been rotated around the brothels attached to military installations in Syria. The risk of sexual disease and the dangers of abortion and childbirth having limited her life expectancy considerably, Turbo spoke to her of sunrises and sunsets, the delicate sound of thunder, and the new of the green in spring.

IIII

Early the next morning, Turbo stood atop the platform roof of the commandant's residence, his hands on the ledge of its terrace. The ballistae were crouched like gigantic sleeping insects, and the sky spread ghostly in the glassy pallor of dawn. One paling star still swam in the shadowy vast.

The trapper's hair was tussled with sleepless night, steel-blond and graying at the temples. His face was hard in the halflight, the lines around his eyes, the wind-chapped lips. His strong jaw and dimpled chin were covered with a frosting of stubble which he would shave later by habit as he did every morning whether with the luxury of razor and lard, or cold water and the blade of his dagger. For thus he preserved the cult of his Roman-ness, regardless of the curly hair and beard brought into fashion by the Antonine and Severan dynasties. As far as he was concerned, the Severans were provincial usurpers, and Marcus Aurelius was excused his on grounds of being a philosopher.

Lucullus watched, and waited. His life had seen considerable reversals of fortune, and yet some things never changed. It would come. Even now Apollo was bridling his steeds, cooing to them as they snorted sleepily, trembling and pawing their great legs awake.

Sunrise in the desert was primeval. There came a rushing upon the horizon. From that first ambiguous reddening under the blue mist at the farthest strip of flatland and sky came great dagger-thrusts across the jagged landscape. The distances were deceiving. The light traveled faster than the wind, blowing black shadows in millions from the nightward surfaces of rocks rippling like nuggets of gold scattered by the gods across the thousands of miles of alkali. And all of that violence, that beauty in action, took place in total silence. Save possibly, when the wind died and the corridors of sound were aligned just right, a soft but powerful, mill-grinding noise of pure energy. Lucullus experienced the sunrise with the strange sensation that a messenger from far and inaccessible abodes had just manifested God to him. Forgotten feelings, pangs of youth quenched long since by the stern service that had been his life, returned strangely metamorphosed.

He watched the Bedouin scouts sleepily mount their camels. Wrapped in voluminous robes, their faces shrouded in scarves against the coming onslaught of sand, they weaved and ducked on the undulating trot of the beasts, penetrating the horizon in that dawning-sun atmosphere of dreams, neither sea nor sky, the earth quite inconsequential. In the latter-day waves of mirage they would seem as if riders of dolphins in a haze of illumined sea.

The legionary vexillations had begun assembling outside of the eastern walls of the city, their centurians barking them into orderly ranks. The renegade ballistae crews arrived on the terrace, crowding around him to watch their comrades depart. Turbo watched the commandant and his staff emerge from Dura's eastern gate on horseback. The men saluted him and bid him good day. As the commandant moved to take his place at the head of the column, he looked to the terrace and met the trapper's far-off gaze.

Lucullus raised his hand and clinched his fist, and the broken man returned the salute and smiled. The garrison on the walls began to clap their hands in time. The sound united and rose to become a crescendo across the river valley. The legionaries on the ground raised their pilums and cheered, and their commandant leveled his hand at the east.

The soldiers wore robes like the Bedouins wore, and the squeaking of the hundreds of carts bearing their gear lurched forth. Only the troops assigned to flanking duty and point were in armor, and these assignments would rotate three times a day as contingents of the XIIth Legion Fulminata, the VIth Ferrata, the Vth Macedonica, and the XVth Apollinaris entered the desert. Noble names all – Thunder, Iron, Macedon and Apollo – Lucullus had mist in his eyes as he watched the dust of their marching begin to rise for miles like a storm in the sky. For he realized what most do not – that nothing is more glorious

than the dreadful pageant of an empire in its
sunset.

V

The barge was a largish, flat-bottomed affair which didn't hold a candle to the ones the trapper rode as a boy on the Nile. But it would do, and the distance he would travel on her wasn't much more than that which he used to travel between the Claudianus Mons and Alexandria, though what took him a week on the Nile would take him two on the Euphrates. Maybe more.

The first thing he ordered done was the removal of its Roman insignia, the defacement of its figurehead, and the haphazard erection of several tents and net-draped palms, anything he could do to make it seem no more than the floating abode of a bizarre band of gypsies. The tents would serve to hide their equipment – the mercenaries' armor and their weapons – and make the barge look like a home, replete with a garden and trees for shade. The men exchanged their clothing for flowing robes, worn and stained with age.

Lucullus' equipment consisted of a fine Scythian bow and its gorytos – a combination quiver and bowcase of silver-plated Greek workmanship. He carried his father's short-sword with the eagle-headed hilt which he wore in a scabbard on his back, and the fat, Spanish-style dagger in his belt. His Nubians loaded the stakes and the heavy netting they would need in the jungle, and then came aboard with their spears and antelope-hide shields. Well aware that Aristotle gave his copy of the 'Iliad' to Alexander, the book the conqueror took with him all the way to India, Turbo had his grandfather's old leather-bound copy of the 'Odyssey.' It was all the poetry he would need.

When the provisions were loaded, the amphorae full of water and wine, the sacks of barley and dried meat he'd purchased from the commissary at Dura, the Nubians sat staring at the Syrians and sharpening their knives. The mercenaries grouped on the other side of the barge, picking lice from their beards and pondering advantages of deception and surprise. Lucullus didn't mind; he liked a little edge with his breakfast, which consisted of yogurt and honey from the sacchari reed, a gourd of water and a few dates before he donned a self-made turban, grabbed a long thrusting pole and yelled at the men to cut the bullshit and put some back into it.

The current was smooth, if a bit slow, and the early autumn weather was warm, but pleasant, with raking sunlight and the moon rising in the east through the azure sky. Dura slid away from them and with her his depression. It was good to be on the move.

After a few miles, he noticed the mercenary captain sitting and sneering with a few of his men, unwilling to row. He pretended to walk past the man and then quickly pivoted and kicked him in the sternum as hard as he could. "I said row, cocksucker," Turbo said softly, looking down at him.

The mercenaries touched the pommels of their swords in momentary confusion, the Nubians quickly drawing their spears. No one moved. The Syrian was fighting tears as he tried to control his inability to breathe, for the fine hard Spanish leather of Lucullus' boot sandal had closed his diaphragm in a knot which would take weeks to fully heal. He nodded at his men to give himself time to think, and stay alive; and the three who sat around him rose slowly to their feet and moved laterally away from the trapper to take up oars.

Lucullus clicked his tongue in annoyance. "Don't forget you're on the payroll," he said, and then moved away to give the man his dignity. After a quarter of an hour, the Syrian weakly took an oar.

The trapper manned the rudder and kept himself in the back of the barge as he did in the taverns on the eastern coasts of the Mediterranean. He would do his best to keep the bastard and his men in front of him for the rest of the journey, and his blacks would know what to do as far as sleep duties. He smiled at the thought of four hundred miles of this. But it was nothing new. This was the East and, after all, nobody had invited him here. And neither had anyone forced on him his chosen profession.

After several days, the river moved out of the rocky desert into a land crisscrossed by a tracery of smaller streams and long-derelict irrigation canals, where towns of burnished mud-brick sat ruined on high mounds above the emerald-green flood plain. Lucullus smiled to himself. Mesopotamia. Once the rich, populous heart of civilization, they saw no one save a few Sand People, wandering aimlessly through the sun-burnt reeds which lined the banks.

The incident of the kicking had seemed to pass, though the trapper knew that was only illusion. He would have to kill the captain in time. But he needed him to be the representative for Moas at Uruk.

When the weather was fair, the river wide and the stars bright, they pushed on through the night, taking shifts at the rudder. If the weather was hazy, and the mist thick off the river, they slept at anchor in her midst, for the Sand People could become curious if given a reason. But it was on those most lucid of nights when he held the rudder, and the heavens shined brightly, that Lucullus reveled in an aloneness that at other times fairly bled him. The trapper had his own brand of misery from being alone too long; and knowing that he would probably die from the cold in the arms of a nightmare, well-aware that his best days were gone. But then he would remember a line from Marcus Aurelius, and watch the stars as if he turned with them. Sometimes one of them would drop off and race obliquely away from its brothers, and he would feel a strange kinship to it, and wonder to himself what could be happening up there.

On the fifth night they passed a fork in the river where part of the Euphrates branched southeast to join the Tigris at Baghdad, and Turbo knew that they'd reached the critical point when, for the next hundred miles or so, they would be within half that distance of the Persian. He had no confusion as to the stars that kept him southwest, however, and they came upon Neapolis in the darkest hours of the night before dawn.

Another of the cities founded by the Seleucids, one of the successor kingdoms of Alexander the Great, most of them were either abandoned after Pompey's annexation of Syria three hundred years before, or assimilated by the Parthians, who moved west in the same period. The depredations of the last war with Rome were evident, and they slid in silence past the broken sandstone peristyles lining the burned-out warehouses of its wharves, with no one save an old hermit wizard watching them from the reed-shuttered doorway of his riverside shack. To the southeast on the horizon, Turbo was momentarily confused by what he thought was the sunrise, only to realize that it was the fires burning in Ctesiphon. He stood holding the rudder with his fine Scythian bow in his free hand, his gorytos slung over his shoulder as he listened to a distant sound of horses on the move, barely perceptible between lulls in the song of the wind in the bulrushes.

VI

The following afternoon, they rounded a bend in the muddy green river and saw great ramparts rising in the distance. Though old and crumbling, their burned brick gleamed like bronze in the hazy autumn sunlight, which illumined the fog off the river like a diaphanous veil through which they seemed to be floating. The tops of stepped pyramids were visible above the crumbling walls, and the cedar-columned porticoes of great temples, their copper-tiled rooftops rippling in the sunlight.

An intricate network of canals began to spread around the barge, silted and overgrown with vegetation. The ruins of pleasure pavilions dotted the canals, summer places rampant with trees and vines and millions of pomegranates, burst and dripping with over-ripeness. The wild overgrowth exuded a rank scent of rot and decay and lay blanketed with the humid fog which roiled out across the river from the stagnant canals along with clouds of mosquitoes and flies.

As they neared the walls of the city, Lucullus could make out the fabled Gate of Ishtar hovering above the overgrowth, its massive face of glazed blue tiles weathered and chipped and run with oxidation, its inlay of gilt sphinxes, bulls and chimeras flaked and blackened, yet still glowing softly. Across the bend in the river he saw the huge raised platform of the palace built by Nebuchadnezzar, its immense walls rising from the water in bands of blue, black and red-enameled brickwork, its portals of bronze stripped and flaking, and dangling impotently from rusted hinges.

The city was still a long way off but there was no mistaking her . . . 'that great whore who sitteth on many waters, with whom the kings of the earth have committed fornication . . .' the barge broke the lazy water as the River Euphrates curved through the ghostly remnants of the fabled Hanging Gardens of ancient Babylon. The colorfully rusting hulks of festival barges rose from the surface of the river, creeper-clad and caked with moss, and the slow-moving current broke peacefully around them.

Mystified by the scene, all rot and jungle and nature run wild, the reclamation of a kingdom by its one-time servitor, Lucullus could see the overgrown ruins of elaborate moat walls, where certain sections of the gardens had been sunken, their lush fruit trees, huge date palms, oaks and tamarisks once watered by elaborate piping systems that gushed water from above.

Thirty yards off their starboard side the remnants of a pleasure pavilion suddenly exploded in a geyser of water and splintered brick that shot laterally over the river and peppered the barge. The men flung themselves on the deck, Lucullus rolling for his bow in a white-hot surge of adrenaline as something very large dopplered over their heads in a screaming whisper and then plunged into a stagnant canal behind them with a powerful sickly thunk that sent great gouts of green slime pluming into the sky to fall in muddy splats over the deck.

The mercenaries glanced back and forth at each other in terror and the Nubians, who were highly superstitious, began to show the whites of their eyes. Lucullus stood with his bow drawn, feeling faintly ridiculous as he faced the huge walls still several hundred yards out. His mind raced for answers but could arrive at no conclusions. Another shrieking devil whipped blasting through a copse of twisted trees to the left of the barge, shattering branches and diving with a painful urgency into the marshy earth. Huge fig leaves helioplaned lazily through the dank air.

"Row like hell, men!" the trapper yelled, grabbing an oar and plunging it into the river, his face in a wild-eyed sneer of grit teeth and sweat. "Forward!"

The men obeyed, imbued with the urgency of their situation; they plunged their oars and rocked their bodies and the barge picked up speed. Several other lightning-fast wind demons flew over their heads, making them all duck and scream; yet they continued their rowing, while the invisible shades tore through trees, into canals, and shattered the remnants of fanciful walls. Not one given to night-time frightenings or petty superstitions, Lucullus' fast-working brain came to the conclusion that there was only one thing that could do what was being done around them, and that was a full-sized Roman ballista, like the ones on the walls at Dura.

"Who's doing the shooting up there!" he yelled at the top of his lungs.

They were nearing the docks now, long stretches of brick-piered ruins, some with the remnants of festival boats and pleasure barges still cobwebbed and rotting between.

"I'm a Roman and a free man, by the gods, and I mean to have an answer!" Turbo continued, the ballistae coming into view atop the walls flanking the gate. Then he felt himself as if in a dream-state when he beheld, out of nowhere, a short fat man running toward them in a white tunic with red Greek-key motif lacing its borders.

"Thought I heard a civilized tongue! Look out, friends, I'm sure!" the little man hopped and shouted. "Don't mind them," he pointed up at the walls, "they get excited when visitors come round!"

The trapper was digging in on the rudder, the barge careening toward a ruined stretch of dock. "Who the hell are you?" he yelled back at the funny fat apparition.

"Lentullus Batiatus," the man stopped up short and saluted. Then he continued his dash and grabbed up a length of rusty chain. "At your service, I'm sure." He promptly slipped on the wet dock and fell on his rear in a seated posture.

The barge slammed into the side of the old dock, gouging loose a few shards of rotten wood, and the little fat man, who had sprung up just as quickly as he fell, threw the big chain clattering onto the deck. He had a round ruddy face with bulging eyes, a bulbous nose and a bald pate with curly gray hair protruding faintly from the sides.

"Who the hell are they?" Lucullus pointed at the walls, bow still in hand.

"Oh that's the goats," the man shrugged, as if speaking of ill-behaved pets.

The Syrians looked nervous and out of their element and the Nubians were confused. One of them quickly ran the chain around several tie-off points on the flank of the barge and their master jumped ashore, slinging the scabbard with his short sword over his back.

"Don't mind them," the little fat man gestured apologetically, "they're just glad to see somebody, I'm sure."

Again the whistling death across the sky and Lucullus ducked and the mercenaries hit the deck and the Nubians scurried fifty yards inland as a section of dilapidated dock on the other side of the river erupted in a blossom of brick chunks and wooden planks cartwheeling up into the air.

Batiatus sighed and wiped the sweat from his pasty brow as the debris pattered down across a large stretch of water. He turned and shouted at the top of the walls, "Come on, boys; that'll do!" and then looked back apologetically at the trapper and shrugged again. Turning back to the walls, "If you shoot up all your bolts," he projected in the tone of a helpless schoolmaster,

"You won't have any bolts left to shoot now, will you?"

The fat little man sighed and shrugged again and Lucullus realized that the men on the walls were members of the IVth Legion Scythica which the commandant's adjutant at Dura had mentioned, saying he had no idea of their status. The emblem of the Scythica was the Capricorn. The Galloping Goat.

"Come along then, I'm sure," Batiatus shrugged and turned and began to waddle down the grand processional way toward the tremendous city gate.

Lucullus looked slowly around him, and then wiped his mouth with the back of his hand in a rare gesture of indecision. He was hesitant to leave the barge and their gear, and the commandant's adjutant at Dura had told them not to stop. But it was getting on evening and his curiosity was piqued. And he was not a little interested in seeing a city which had been the center of the civilized world for three thousand years.

"Boat should be fine," the little fat man called out, as if reading his thoughts. "No worries, I'm sure," he continued as he waddled down the thoroughfare. "Sand People don't come round much," he waved his hand dismissively. "Scared of the Goats."

The trapper hesitated a moment longer and then nodded at the mercenary captain, who duly motioned for his men to gather their gear.

"Go easy with those spears, friends," Batiatus shouted back. "Might carry them over your backs, keep them pretty relaxed," he went on. "Goats don't take too kindly to your skin-tone, I'm afraid." He shrugged again, his back to them as he waddled toward the gate. "Should be all right, though. No worries I'm sure. Come along then. Come, come."

The mercenaries were evident in their blue tunics, leather trousers, boots and Arabic complexions. They didn't speak more than a few words of Latin, but their captain translated. As far as Lucullus could see, it wasn't really necessary; for the Syrians looked pale enough that he wondered if they were really worth their salt in the first place. He nodded to his Nubians and leveled his hand at the ground. In tune to the most infinite indications in his physical bearing, the blacks dismissed their superstitions and set off at his bidding, flanking the roadside beneath a row of palm trees.

The grand processional way led from the river wharves to the Gate of Ishtar; a hundred yards of highway through gardens gone to seed, its corridor of flanking palms dripping with gigantic vines that, in some places, had reached the ground and taken root. Lucullus came up level with Batiatus, who was hopping nimbly over the cracks in the massive paving stones. "Do you mind telling me what's going on here?" he asked.

"I thought you were going to tell me that," the fat little man laughed in reply.

The trapper looked at him.

"You mean you're not," Batiatus said, taking as much care as he could of his red velvet sandals with the closed toe and heel housings, which looked to have been repatched more than a few times. "You're not from High Command?"

"High Command?" Lucullus smiled despite himself. "What the hell is that? Do we look like it?"

"Well nothing looks like it's supposed to anymore," the little fat man smiled back poignantly.

The trapper couldn't help but agree.

"Not from Dura," continued Batiatus, more to himself than Lucullus, shaking his head and smiling.

"Came by there," the trapper replied. "On my way south."

"Are they coming for us?" the little man looked up expectantly.

Lucullus shook his head. "I think they have their hands full."

"Oh."

They passed the remnants of elaborate altars on raised platforms where priests in golden robes once burned incense and oil to waft pleasant smells across the triumphal entries of kings and prelates. The steps leading to the altars were cracked and rife with weeds and large blossoming roots that had grown up through them and split the joins between, and the statues were cracked and dripping with vines.

"Right then," Batiatus went on, changing the subject and trying cheerfully to make conversation. "What are you doing here, if you don't mind my asking?"

"Little trading on the river," Lucullus replied, turning to check the progress of his men. The Nubians were moving steadily up the roadside, the Syrians coming with infinitely less discipline from behind, their eyes on the walls atop which the men of the Fourth Scythica were staring at them.

"I didn't catch your name," the little fat man asked.

"I didn't throw it," responded the trapper.

"Right."

They walked on a bit further, past a row of tremendous statues of fanciful bulls, all neck, shoulders and flanks. Batiatus asked, "What sort of trading do you do?"

"Lucullus Turbo," the trapper sighed. "I'm in animals."

"Animals yes, well." And then his eyes rolled in thought. "Turbo you say? . . . hm . . ." he scratched his balding pate of curly gray hair. "That name sounds familiar." He thought for a second longer and then raised a short pudgy finger, "I've got it now. Lacus Curtius Turbo!"

"My grandfather."

"Fine man he was too, old boy," the little fat man snapped his finger, pleased with himself, his eyes bulging with excitement.

"I didn't really know him," the trapper replied, his eyes out watching the very strange figures of Roman legionaries milling about under the trees flanking the roads and seemingly devoid of any kind of concentrated purpose.

"Shame that is, lad. Don't make them like him anymore. Did business on a handshake," his eyes bulged. "No need for a contract with old Turbo," his jowls shook enthusiastically. "Roman to the bone. Wouldn't waste money on lawyers and all that mess. Yes, well," he smiled, "You come well recommended, my boy," gripping the trapper's muscled shoulder with his pudgy little hand. "Turbo," he nodded with a smile.

From the watery memory of being taken to see his grandfather at his offices in Trastevere at the age of four while on one of their trips to Rome, Lucullus vaguely recalled him as a stern businessman with little patience for children. He turned back to Batiatus. "If you don't mind my saying so, you look a little out of place here," he said. "Do you mind my asking what you're doing?"

"Oh that," laughed Batiatus. "That's easy. I'm in the shipping business."

"Ah."

"Your grandfather taught me everything I know," he smiled proudly, his face touchingly sincere.

"Small world," nodded Lucullus.

"Yes, well," Batiatus glanced up at him, "unfortunately it seems to be getting a bit smaller," his eyes rolled a bit in his head, "if you get my drift, old boy."

The trapper grunted, walking along, still puzzled at the soldiers scattered out through the trees. "Anybody in charge here?"

"Seleucian wall panels, Babylonian altarpieces," began the fat little man, his jowls shaking again with enthusiasm, "all the rave in Rome. Set a new style in villa decoration. The Parthians were fairly giving the stuff away," his eyes bulged with pleasure at the thought. "I was the direct connection for the Emperor's personal decorator. The former one, that is."

Lucullus didn't know whether he meant the former emperor, or former decorator. "Anybody in charge here?," he asked again.

"Oh him," Batiatus nodded curtly. "Well he's," he seemed to search for the word, "he's a poet," he concluded, nodding. "And a bit of a salty dog as well, old boy."

"Who?"

"Well, the commander, I'm sure," the little man nodded again.

Lucullus turned his head and looked at him. "I want to speak with this commander."

"Animals, you say?" queried Batiatus, avoiding the subject. "Fine trade," he nodded, as if it passed the test. "Following in your grandfather's footsteps, I'm sure."

"More or less."

VII

The Gate of Ishtar, the ancient Sumerian god of the North Star, rose before them like a cliff face. Huge streaks of black oxidation ran downward from the seams of its monstrous gilt inlays. The overall impression of blue-glazed brick from a distance was overturned upon close inspection by the gate's age-subtled polychrome friezes of griffons, eagles and lions bordered in geometric patterns of colored stone. Half a dozen legionaries stood about in the shadows beneath the tremendous rotting portcullis which hung precariously from the top half of the gate's fifty-foot pointed archway. The men were in various states of uniform, subarmilii with head dresses, some in leather armor. They seemed subdued in the same strange way that Lucullus had noticed in those scattered out amongst the trees flanking the grand processional street. By their eyes, the trapper guessed opium.

"Hey Baty," one of the legionaries asked softly, glancing at the line of Nubians and the mercenaries, "is that a circus there you brung us?"

"Careful there, boys. These are friends. Here in the service of Rome."

"Service of Rome," another of them said, widening his eyes and smiling vacuously.

"Just like them dancers you brung up, hey Baty?" one in a head dress said quietly. "Old Baty always treats us right, don't you?"

"And those ballistae bolts with the incendiary housings," said the first of them. "When you bring us some more of those?"

"Business is slow right now, lads," the little fat man replied patiently. "You know that."

"I thought you were in the art trade," Lucullus said, glancing at him.

Batiatus shrugged and smiled helplessly, "Well I dabble, old boy. I dabble," wiping his ruddy face with a handkerchief. "Times are hard, you know."

The gate's interior was lined with the ruined booths that had once housed merchants, money-changers, taxationists and petty vendors. Lucullus noticed a trio of legionaries with their backs against the wall, the middle one loading a chunk of mud-colored hashish into an old Aramaic hookah. He passed through the cavernous corridor to emerge into one of the oldest, most famous cities in the world in a state of magnificently abandoned decay. Some of her great buildings still stood, derelict temples and ziggurats, as did her walls in many places, wide enough to drive chariot teams along their battlemounts.

"Most areas you don't want to go," said Batiatus, as they walked across the grand square inside the Gate of Ishtar, "these days. When Artabanus was still in power, the place had a thriving tour business. The Parthian kings

71

entertained guests here and used it as a resort. Some of the gardens were even patched up," he smiled.

The square was lined with huge, curly-bearded gods in stiff sandstone poses ranked between palm and fig trees in tremendous vases. Several of the colossal statues had fallen, and lay split open, their oriental eyes the size of watermelons staring in silence through the tapestry of withered leaves and yellowed fronds littering the pavement. The trees were mostly dead, and some of their vases had cracked and burst as well, spilling trunks and dried dirt across the square.

Lucullus looked up and behind him at the ballistae mounted on the wide platforms atop the walls. The artillery pieces were on rollers, and could be pulled into different positions relatively easily. It seemed as if the leftover garrison, a remnant of a peacekeeping and police force established after the last Parthian war ten years ago, had fortified a corner of the city within the walls after the Sassanid uprising in order to await either relief or a last stand.

"The city had ten quarters," the little fat man continued, assuming the air of a tour guide, "each with its own gate. Twenty-four great boulevards," he said, gesturing down the one that led from the Gate of Ishtar, where weeds grew up to five and six feet in some places between the huge paving stones.

Lucullus could see barricades in the distance, formed by collapsed buildings and rubble. Catapults had been positioned behind them, with flaming cauldrons at hand to light their shot.

"Forty-three temples of the old Seleucian gods," Batiatus shook his jowls with enthusiasm. "Most of them have been in disrepair since the Persian occupation under Xerxes six hundred years ago, but can you imagine the gold-mine still to be had, old boy? Nine hundred chapels of the lesser gods!" his eyes bulged at the thought of so much lost commerce. "Crying shame it is, crying shame," he gestured in lament. "Hundreds more neighborhood shrines. The Parthian royal family was selling it for a song! Haven't even scratched the surface, I'm sure."

"I take it you're not overly religious," Lucullus said.

"The garrison is grouped around the palace here in the northern sector," Batiatus continued. "Don't want to go trashing about over there, old boy," he said, noticing the trapper's gaze, which was directed out over the distant rooftops to where the great Temple of Etemkenanki loomed in vast swathes of shadow in the declining sunlight. "The Crazies come out at night," the little fat man explained.

Blackened with age and dotted with isolated pockets of flame, the massive ziggurat appeared to have taken more than a few random ballistae hits.

"They got a couple of the Goats last week," Batiatus continued. "We picked them up in the morning," he shook his head sadly, "wasn't much left of them, poor lads."

The trapper noticed one of the mail-skirted legionary archers behind the barricade at the end of the boulevard dip an arrow with an incendiary bulb into a cauldron of flame, draw back slowly, and arc the point of fire up into the misty autumn afternoon.

"The Persians are already in the eastern districts," said the little fat man.

Lucullus raised an eyebrow.

"They don't really seem to be coordinated, old boy," Batiatus went on, as if to reassure him. "Probably just slaves from Ctesiphon and the tenant farmers caught short in the fall-out, poor wretches. Goats got the catapults going night and day, whenever they feel like it really. But," his bug eyes rolled a bit as if divulging a secret, "probably best for us all to be pulling up stakes here soon. If you get my drift, that is."

Approaching the city-side entrance of the ancient Palace of Nebuchadnezzar, Lucullus recalled with a certain melancholy awe that this was the building in which Alexander the Great, after his return from India, had died of stress, sadness and fever at the age of thirty-two, after seeking to medicate his losses through herculean bouts of drinking with his subalterns. From its foot in the square bordering the Gate of Ishtar, they began their ascent of the grand staircase, picking their way through groups of bandaged legionaries, some drugged or drinking wine, staring at them with large, vacuous eyes. The tremendous bronze oil braziers flanking the staircase were still in place, rusted hulks with elaborate systems of cobwebs lacing their stands.

Batiatus huffed and puffed and hitched his tunic to give his thick little legs room to climb, and the Nubians and the Syrian mercenaries followed warily from behind. The massive square portal was flanked by unmanned ballistae on either side, and one of its giant bronze-encased cedar-wood doors had fallen inward from its huge rotted hinges. The group circumvented the mass of the fallen door to pass through the portal into the halflight of an enormous audience hall.

Columns thundered across the distance. Though fifty feet tall, the columns were so thick that they appeared to be squat. Inlayed with colored stone, copper and mother of pearl, the sandstone shafts upheld a ceiling beamed in spans that could have only been reached by cedars of the Lebanon, some cracked and shorn up with scaffolding in repairs that were abandoned decades ago. Remnants of pavilions and raised platforms grouped about the tens of thousands of square feet of space, where kings and prelates once sat in audience on the great king himself. The walls were composed of massive glazed-brick reliefs, and through the half-light Lucullus could make out ranks of archers, infantry and heavy cavalry passing in train, each of the figures thirty feet tall. Huge doorways around the walls led into a maze of corridors and antechambers leading off the audience hall, and on the center of the long wall was an altar-like throne with stairs leading to a platform where the King of Babylon once sat in court flanked by a frieze of griffons under the winged disc of Ahura Mazda, god of illumination.

Rampant with the ghosts of a marvelously archaic past, the audience hall's current inhabitants were the legionary garrison, whose dozens of large gauze tents were arranged haphazardly around the huge columns and pavilions to keep the mosquitoes off them when they slept. Cooks had begun the evening meal, and Lucullus and crew followed Batiatus across the space through its huge forest of massive colorful columns over its vast rotting rugs past the isolated, stone-bordered fires with cauldrons atop them and sheep turning roasting on spits. They reached another grand staircase in the corner of the room that led up through its ceiling, which they ascended into a space not much smaller than the one below it.

The second-level hall was full of what looked like ancient astronomical instruments. Tarnished bronze globes and slide rules with segmented arcs, huge apparati bigger than the ballistae atop the walls, the instruments appeared to have been moved there many years ago for safekeeping or storage and then forgotten. Lucullus was familiar with the systems of Philolaus and Hipparchus, and he'd seem similar machinery in the laboratories at the Mouseion of

Alexandria where he attended university amidst the hushed clashes of opinion and the competitiveness of inventive minds.

"I found stacks of the astronomical records of the old Babylonian priests," said Batiatus. "Shelf after cobwebbed shelf containing knowledge supposedly going back thirty thousand years," his eyes bulged and his jowls trembled. "All written in cuneiform and just sitting their rotting. Fetch a pretty penny at auction, I'm sure." He shook his head. "Crying shame it is, crying shame."

The four walls were a series of open bays through which square pylons were spaced widely apart. The rings which once hung vast sweeping draperies were still intact; and in the morning and the evening, with the sun horizontal, their golden-dyed swathes of linen would have filtered a heavenly light. The bays looked out over the city and the gardens and the verdant floodplain beyond. To the east the rooftops of Babylon, to the west a splendid view of the river and quay walls. To the north the famous Hanging Gardens, and to the south the continuation of the Euphrates toward the Persian Gulf. Lucullus ordered his Nubians and the mercenaries to await him there, as he followed Batiatus up another smaller staircase in the corner of the room.

"The commander's a bit under the weather these days," said Batiatus. "Don't know quite what you're expecting but . . . well he's . . . he means well, old boy, he means well."

VIII

They passed a rectangle in the ceiling and came onto an observation deck, where a bald man sat in a curule chair with a fragment of ancient tapestry covering him like a blanket. The man was large and bull-necked and, when Batiatus cleared his throat to announce their arrival, he did not move. Two legionaries stood at opposite ends of the platform, which stretched a hundred feet on each side and was planted with spears about its ledge. On each of the spears was a severed head. The heads were in more or less recent states of severance, and most had the typical thick, curly beard and dressed hair of the Persian.

The little fat man cleared his throat, "I say there, sir. I have someone here who would like to speak with you," he said. "Comes from noble Roman stock."

The man elevated his head slightly but did not turn it. They arrived in front of him and his eyes, fever-ridden and slightly wild, looked up at them.

Batiatus fetched one of the fold-out camp chairs leaning against the wall of a small room which rose in the center of the observation deck, where the commander presumably resided. He placed the chair at Lucullus' disposal. "Well, I'll be taking my leave now," he nodded at the commander. "We'll speak later," he said to the trapper, who remained standing, his eyes out south along the Euphrates, where the Gulf and his goal of India lay beyond.

"You're welcome to sit down," the bald man said. Though obviously dying of fever, he exuded a latent physical power, a sense which the trapper had felt in the presence of the best Greek sculpture, and of big game in repose. "You might stay a bit down-wind, however. I've moved myself up here so I wouldn't stink my men out. No sense upsetting the lads."

Lucullus opened the chair, placed it beside him and sat. The sweet stink of death pervaded the space between.

"What's your name?" the man asked quietly, without looking at him.

"Turbo," the trapper replied. He cleared his throat. "Sir."

"Where are you from, Turbo?"

"I was born in Rome, but raised in Egypt."

"Egypt," the man repeated distantly, his eyes somewhere out across the eastern horizon where tendrils of smoke rose through the orange haze. "I remember a trip up the Nile River with my parents when I was a boy," he smiled softly. "It was spring, and the banks were lined with huge water lilies, all of them in bloom," he spoke slowly, and seemed to strain with the memory. "The air was perfumed with an exotic scent . . . that I have never since experienced the like of."

79

The trapper squinted his eyes, but did not look at the man.

The commander dipped a rag into a bowl of water by his side and brought it to his head, where the water trickled in rivulets down its clean-shaven surface and over his smooth brow. "Have they sent you," he asked quietly, the water dripping from his aquiline nose, "to revoke my command, Turbo?"

Lucullus squinted slightly. "No." He cleared his throat again. "Sir. They've sent me on a mission to trap game for the Arena."

"The Arena. I see."

Darkness was settling in and the scattered flames in the distance brightening into pinpoints of white light.

"Do you believe the Arena," the commander put his hands to his temples, "to be a justified sacrifice of life, Turbo?" He rubbed his eyebrows and pinched his nose where the water had slightly tickled it.

The trapper gazed out across the city, a multi-leveled pastiche of terraced rooftops run amok with foliage, towers with bulbous tops, stepped pyramids and temples.

"I'm not sure," he replied, "that I've ever seen a justified sacrifice of life, sir. I know only that everything has to die."

"Perhaps you're right," the bald man nodded. "After all . . . what separates us," he gestured casually at the severed heads topping the spears around the observation deck, "from the screaming of grass when it's cut?"

Lucullus looked across the rank of heads staring in drowsy shock out over the void. Blood and gore had coagulated like sap at the bases of the jagged throats, and small particles of it hung dried in the act of dripping.

Time passed. An orderly arrived and filled the commander's bowl with fresh water. "Dominus," he nodded. Another brought a tripod table with a pitcher of wine and two cups, basic clay military issue. The men were young and of Italic descent, and wore red tunics belted at the waist.

When they left, Lucullus lifted the pitcher of wine to fill the commander's cup, but the bald man raised several fingers from the armrest of his chair. He had the rare ability to make even his smallest gestures seem important, and by it the trapper knew that he had declined the wine.

Lucullus poured for himself. "I'll be heading south on the river in the morning. Do you have any information about the toll station at Uruk?"

Perhaps the oldest city in the world, predating Babylon by two thousand years, Uruk's windswept ruins had served as the site of a Seleucid, and then a Parthian, toll station for the river traffic coming from the Persian Gulf.

"I doubt there is a functioning toll station at Uruk anymore," the commander replied softly. "Commerce has stopped for the recent uprising, and there is no reason for anyone to bother with maintaining a toll station. If there is," he went on, "it will no doubt be in the hands of tribal brigands or even, possibly, the Sassanid Persian." He raised his fingers slightly, "if they're trying to outflank us to the south."

Lucullus felt his stomach muscles tighten infinitely. Not with fear, but anger. For though he had trained himself to the philosophy of Stoicism, he was rapidly reaching a point where he had to make a decision upon whether to purchase elephants and rhino at all, or simply gather what he could take back on the monsoon ships, which would vastly reduce his profit in Rome.

"Each time that the Parthians have sued for peace with us," the commander stated, "their chief concern has been the reopening of the trade routes between Rome and India, and the Land of Silk beyond. In this, the Jewish merchants and the Arab exporters have been of no little assistance." He placed the wet rag to his head. "And yet we have always been dependent upon the Parthians, for they have always held the franchise for the roads and ports."

Given his business, Lucullus knew it only too well. Trajan had conducted the peace conferences with Osroes, the Parthian king, right here in the Palace at Babylon after his sack of Ctesiphon a century before. And though the emperor had forced the Parthians to return the Roman standards captured at Carrhae a century and a half prior, which they had subsequently adorned their temples with, the real discourse was conducted at tables lined with Arabs in flowing head dresses and Jews in black robes.

And the issue was always trade routes and commerce.

"Our great expeditions in these parts," continued the commander, gesturing halfheartedly out into the blood-red Mesopotamian twilight, "have simply been efforts to dispense with this loosely joined alliance of satrapies – of Armenians, Parths, Medes, Elymaics and Persians which grew out of the primordial civilizations of the Hittites, Assyrians, Babylonians and Sumerians – in order to touch directly upon the rich extremities of the world." He smiled softly, and shook his head. "The problem of the Orient has preoccupied us for centuries."

Lucullus recalled the legend that two out of the seven Roman legions destroyed at Carrhae were actually captured by the Parthians, and subsequently used on their own eastern frontiers beyond the Aral Sea in warfare against the Empire of Silk. One of the soldiers had supposedly made his way back to Rome in old age with an amazing green stone, like a diamond, or a star, which was housed in the temple of the Earth Mother Goddess on the Palatine Hill.

"There is no concept of the benefit of Rome here, Turbo," the commander said after a time. "Of what we would provide in terms of a unified scheme of administration, from which everyone would collectively benefit," he nodded, his fingers lifting infinitely. "There is no concept here of Roman justice . . . or order," he pronounced the words as if they were sacraments, "here." And then he turned his head slightly and looked at the trapper. "The women scream with their tongues, by Mithras," he said softly, squinting his eyes.

Lucullus glanced at him.

The man's pupils looked like black holes in the sky.

"Even now, Turbo," he continued, as if relaying a vision, "the Parthian royal family in Ctesiphon kneels in chains to watch their former vassals repeatedly rape their wives and daughters. Even now," he repeated quietly, "less than one hundred miles from here," raising his thick arm and pointing at the horizon to the northeast, which pulsed in the growing darkness. "They burn our prisoners alive," he nodded. "We slaughter theirs," he shook his head slightly, "for lack of ability to transfer them to the slave auctions in Palestine."

The trapper remembered from his history lessons at Alexandria that Ctesiphon had grown out of ancient Seleucia, to become the functioning Parthian capital for hundreds of years. The Romans razed its imperial palace twice, once under Trajan. The second time, under Marcus Aurelius, the victory was more costly than defeat; for it was then that the legions caught the plague which had begun to rage throughout Mesopotamia, and brought it back through Europe, where it swept devastation. Now Ctesiphon was burning again and Baghdad, its sister-city a hundred miles due north on the same river, was also firmly in Persian hands.

"The burning," the commander said, "the looting," speaking softly, "and the . . . Kaos" he whispered, using the Greek word, "will go on for a time, Turbo. It is the way of the world."

"The question," nodded Lucullus, "is for how long?"

"Oh it will go on," the commander nodded. "And on . . . and on, and on . . . " he smiled. "Until the earth is cleansed by fire . . . and then renewed."

The trapper's eyes focused on a tiny flaming catapult shot careening wildly off over ruined Babylonian apartment blocks.

"Ardashir is in Ctesiphon," the commander said, his coal-black eyes somewhere out on the pulsing northeastern horizon, "part of his army besieging Hatra with the objective of Dura next." He dipped his rag into the bowl of water, and brought it slowly to his brow. "If he succeeds, it will effectively cut off our reinforcements from Europe." The water ran in rivulets down his nose, chin and cheeks. "We, however, are already cut off."

Lucullus cleared his throat. "You could break out, sir."

There was silence for a time.

"I've served Rome all of my adult life, Turbo" the commander smiled softly. "I was tribune in Germany, senior tribune in Gaul . . . and a legatus in Britain," he nodded, squeezing the rag over his forehead, "I was prefect in Judaea," he raised his chin and thrust it forth, and then returned his strange, sweating orb of a head to normal, "some years ago." He leaned over and grasped the pitcher of wine.

"The governor of Syria had me ordered back to Rome to stand trial for crimes in office," he admitted, pouring himself a cup, the tapestry falling from his arm. "I'd killed a few Jews," he opened his hand in a throw-away gesture, as of a farmer scattering chaff in the wind.

Lucullus saw commotion and heard shouts at a distant intersection where a tongue of flame licked across the street.

"They were typical insurrectionists, Turbo," the commander shrugged slightly. "My nightly reports just as predictable. Two legionaries drinking in a tavern knifed in the back . . . road detail hailed with projectiles, four dead. Medallions of the emperor continuously defaced . . . throwing rocks and camel shit at my guards." He placed the cup of wine on the table without drinking from it.

"I suppose some of us would call them murderous, religious fanatics." He angled his head. "I found it quite natural in fact. Despite the dubious honor conveyed upon them as an . . . 'Official Province of Roma Urbis,'" he smiled sadly.

"The Christians pushed it over the edge," he nodded, lifting several fingers. "It happened to be one of those capricious months when they were declared by the emperor to be official . . . what was it . . . 'Enemies of the State,'" he stated, still smiling softly. "In reality, they were probably the best of his subjects there. They paid their taxes, they obeyed the laws. They didn't take their subjugation personally like the zealots who hated them for it.

Lucullus continued to watch the distant intersection, where the tongue of flame bisecting it was burning low. He noticed several figures run past and leap across it, black shadows against its glow.

"We'd rounded some of them up and I'd had them flogged. Then I freed them, showed them good old Roman leniency," the commander raised an eyebrow. "If anyone there deserved it, it was those unfortunate sheep." He took a sip of wine, inclined his head, and seemed to savor the effects of its volcanic mystery on his raging fever.

"But when they walked out of the Praetorium that day, the stripes of my flogging still running blood down their backs," he touched his brow with the base of his palm, "the Jews who'd insisted upon their incarceration went insane," his hissed softly, his fist clenching slowly as he lowered it to the armrest of his chair. "They stoned them to death in my own forecourt. Right under my nose." His lips curled into a sneer.

The moon had begun to rise on the eastern horizon. Still illumined by the sun's last defracted rays, it hung a massive burnished rose, its size emphasized by its proximity to the horizon. A red moon over Mesopotamia, pocketed with craters, ripped with ejectile scars and broken by the silhouette of the ziggurat of Etemenkanki.

"I had those murderers quickly dispatched by the members of my guard closest at hand," he shivered softly with fever, and pulled the tapestry tighter around him, a threadbare, moth-eaten beautiful swathe of Seleucian heavy weaving. "The situation quickly became the pebble that set off a landslide, the zealots capitalizing on any excuse to riot, however small," he continued. "The next thing I knew, thousands of them were screaming outside my gates, throwing rocks and pulling their hair out," he smiled again softly. "Like animals, they began to set fire to everything including their own houses," he gestured out over the city, where the reflections of isolated pockets of flame flickered on distant walls.

"I called out the garrison," he shrugged. "Retaliation led to further retaliation . . . until the streets," he raised his head at an angle and thrust out his chin, "were painted with blood."

The fire burning across the distant intersection pulsed lower still, and Lucullus saw a figure, its form distorted by heaps of rags, emerge from a grate in the street carrying a spiked club.

"The governor called it the . . . worst blemish on Roman authority since Titus burned the Temple of Solomon," the commander smiled. "I was charged with," he searched for the technicality, "jeopardizing provincial security."

The trapper continued to watch the tiny ragged figure in the distant intersection below, as he lurched down the avenue through the dying firelight banging his club atop staggered grates ranked down the disance, which presumably accessed a sewer system beneath the street. Other figures such as he emerged with his passing, the grates popping up and sliding aside as they climbed hunchbacked from the holes like dead from their tombs.

"And yet the question remains, Turbo," the bald man nodded. "If one cannot officiate the provinces with Roman . . . Order. With efficiency and justice," he lifted his hand slightly, "why are we here?

The trapper lifted his gaze from the silent macabre into the sky, where a delicate mandala of stars had begun to rise in the northeast like sisters of the Moon, which had shrunk, and cooled with her rising.

"Why are the legions here?" the commander's voice had almost become a whisper.

"I knew only one way to run things," he continued after a time. "The Roman Way," he nodded. "The way I was brought up under. The way I was taught by her. In the end, there is no cultural diversity, Turbo. There are no concessions. There is only . . . Civilization or Kaos. There is only Rome . . . or Darkness." He lifted his hand infinitely from the armrest of his chair. "And yet . . . we can level their cities and burn their citadels . . . but we cannot prevent the

East from answering us," he raised his eyebrows and smiled thinly . . . "'No.'"

"I understand, sir." the trapper replied. It was all he could think of to say.

The two men sat in silence for a while. Lucullus downed several cups of wine in relatively quick succession. Sitting there in his Arab head dress and flowing robe, with his all-too-familiar personal stink weaving in and out of that of the commander's dying one, the wine mixed with his growing fatigue to give him the displaced, and not entirely unpleasant, sensation that he was going very quietly insane.

"Would you accept," the bald man asked after a time, "occupation, Turbo?"

The trapper's gaze roved across the city. The Esagila, the great shrine of the god Marduk, stood in ruins, and the huge ziggurat Temple of Etemenkanki, the famous Tower of Babel atop which legend expounded ritual sex and prostitution with crocodiles, was lit as if with candles about its base from the isolated pockets of flame. "No . . ." he replied. "I wouldn't."

"Oh but you have," the commander stated gently, as if in the presence of a favored schoolboy's mistake on an oral exam. "Even as early as the Julio-Claudians, Turbo, the writer Lucan was bemoaning the fact that Rome was becoming depopulated of its own citizens and filled with the . . . 'dregs of the universe,' as he put it. Why, Nero himself enjoyed mixing with the riffraff of Aramaic courtesans and flute-players who hung around the Circus Maximus."

"But now," the man cocked his head infinitely, "a century and a half later . . . there are Orientals in the Senate, Turbo. In the corridors of power with their fingers in the pots of the Imperial domestic scene." He took a sip from his cup and shivered with its burn. The wine was harsh, and not far from its original communion with the earth.

"From North Africa to the banks of the Rhine and Danube rivers," he said, "Commagenians, Emesians, Ituraeans and Palmyrenians," raising his fingers, "such as those of your own mercenary escort . . . serve as archers, footsoldiers, and cavalrymen in our legions. If you recall, Turbo, Severus conferred citizenship upon all citizens of tax-paying provinces," he inclined his head slightly.

The lurching crazies had grouped and begun a strange slow dancing advance toward a Roman barricade one hundred yards distant.

"Do you understand what this means, Turbo?" the commander asked.

The trapper remained silent.

"It means, quite simply, that the Latin race is being bred out. Bred out of existence."

In response to faint shouts from the barricade, half a dozen legionary archers, tiny figures in head dresses and robes, were jogging towards the barricade.

"My men are all Italics, Turbo. They are Romans," the commander nodded. "Would I relegate them to continue in a world . . . such as this one?" he gestured outward. "Or is it not more . . . ethical . . . to gently lead them toward an honorable exit?"

Lucullus cleared his throat. "Surely their lives are still worth something."

He watched the archers draw back, their powerful, horn-laminated bows effective up to a hundred meters, with a maximum range of two hundred and seventy-five. As they released, half a dozen slow crazies flipped, jerked and spun to stillness, one of them kicking wildly from a fetal position in the street.

"Have you ever considered any . . . real freedoms, Turbo?" asked the commander. "Freedoms from the opinions of others. Freedoms from the opinions of the gods?" he elevated his head. "Freedoms from the opinions of the society which, despite your better judgment, you have sought to conform to since childhood. Freedoms even from the opinions of your Self?" he lowered his head and turned his gaze on Lucullus. "Which is the same thing as the gods, their different personalities simply an indication of your own soul . . . torn apart . . . and crying out in every direction."

The trapper squinted his eyes.

"Did you ever look back on your life," the commander continued, his voice a hoarse whisper, "and wonder if any of it had really mattered?" he smiled.

"I've been in the army all of my life," he continued. "I loved Britain," he cocked his head in that strange manner, as if listening to a voice only he could hear, "the mist-shrouded mornings . . . the witch-haunted evenings . . . ."

"Surely the lives of your men?" Lucullus interrupted.

"Will be renewed . . . like the blades of grass in spring," the commander smiled.

"You could break out," Lucullus repeated quietly, looking straight ahead.

"I have . . . broken out, Turbo," the commander nodded, and then looked at him with those eyes like black holes in the sky. "And this is where I have arrived."

The sounds of revelry rose from below, where the evening meal had, as usual, given way to a stripteased drunken banquet for those of the soldiers not on duty. Lucullus realized that Babylon had become like the long slow party of a religious sect preparing for collective suicide.

"The sun is in the East," the commander concluded, pointing faintly at the pulsing horizon. "Even though the day is done."

"Two suns in the sunset," the trapper smiled softly. And he felt a great lament rise up like bile in his throat.

IX

The next morning the sky was a gray haze into which the bottom half of a yellow sun was disappearing, after having risen through a thin stretch of clear sky across the eastern horizon. The sun's momentary gilding slipped off the blanket of trees and wild vegetation that was all that was left of the fabled Hanging Gardens of Babylon, returning the tops of the city's crumbling walls and buildings to hulking shadow. Lucullus, who had risen before dawn in the room full of astronomical equipment, emerged from the Gate of Ishtar walking down the grand processional way toward the docks with the sounds of fighting picking up in the city over the birdsong shot out through the trees.

"I say, you wouldn't be heading back Tibur-way by any chance, would you, old boy?" asked Batiatus, as he tripped along through the halflight trying to catch up with the trapper.

"Not for a while yet."

"Ah, ah," nodded the little fat man, dismissing the matter, made of sterner stuff.

Lucullus' men and the mercenaries were already at the docks loading the several iron cauldrons and the dozen amphorae full of the flammable oil used to light catapult shot which he'd purchased from the garrison quartermaster, along with the disassembled parts of a small anti-personnel ballista. The trapper had also procured a dozen of the smaller steel bolts with the banded incendiary housings and a like number of bows and quivers full of arrows, some with the wire bulbs below their tips for inserting oil-drenched plugs and setting them alight. At his order, the men began ripping wooden planks off the docks and loading them onto the barge as well.

Horns were sounding the battle alarm from the walls, and the legionaries stationed out among the trees and around the docks were jogging past them toward the city, where an attack from the east was beginning in earnest with the sunrise. The sounds of the catapults were coming now, and the distant shouts of the centurians as they hustled the hungover garrison gathering their gear and tripping down the stairs of the palace toward the barricades.

"Ahem," Batiatus again. "Sorry mate, how long was it you said there, old boy?" scratching the back of his neck and squinting. He had a satchel with his belongings – his corporate seal, contractual parchments and stilus, his needle and thread to repair his sandals – on a strap over his bulging torso.

The trapper turned and looked at him for a moment, a load of ballistae bolts over his shoulder. "Come along with us if you like."

"That's it!" replied the little fat man, fairly hopping. "No sense traveling alone, I always say." His eyes bulged with excitement. "Man needs a civilized conversation over his evening meal, what? And, well, nice to have somebody from your own neck of the woods around from time to time, it is."

A huge ball of fire roared over them and into the far docks and Batiatus jumped six feet onto the deck of the barge where he collapsed to his knees and then popped right up. "I say, you do favor your grandfather, lad! Have his eyes."

Lucullus yelled at the crew to get their gear secured, then leapt gracefully onto the barge, set the ballista bolts down and grabbed a thrusting pole. "Let's get moving!"

The men followed suit and dug their poles, and then oars, into the water. When they reached the center of the river, the trapper walked to the back and took the rudder. He would shave on the way.

The barge slid along the line of ruined quays, past the sweeping bulk of the palace, its terraced platforms run-amok with weeds. Huge archaic statues of seated lions and bulls had cracked and burst open upon its multi-leveled staircases, and its colorfully-enameled brick wall friezes were age-blackened and run with slime. In the southern city districts, stairs grown with foliage led down from the streets to the river banks, where traders had once landed their wares from the Persian Gulf and India beyond. Bundles of rags marked the corpses of crazies that lay in heaps of decomposition across the steps, and a tower of black smoke was roiling up into the overcast from somewhere in the midst of the city sliding by. Lucullus' last vision of Babylon was of flaming catapult shot arcing slowly back and forth above the walls like some bat-and-ball game in Hell.

When they moved out into the widening water highway past the city, the trapper had Batiatus take the rudder while he moved the three cauldrons on iron legs to the front of the barge, away from the tent shacks which were slung low under the stunted palm trees at the back. Then he set about constructing a makeshift ballista of his own, using the stem of the broken-off figurehead on the barge's prow for a fulcrum, hacking it into a short post with his sword, and placing the thick oaken planks to either side of it. He set the elevation platform where the boards sloped down to the deck at an angle, then fit the pegs on the inside of them into the stepped grooves in its stem. He fixed the boards to the hacked-off prow with large spiked pegs, which he hammered with a mallet through the holes designed for them; likewise the elevation post, nailing it to the deck through the holes in its base of iron plate. The pegs allowed the boards the vertical movement they would need while the settings on the elevation post were raised or lowered to control distance, but lateral movement would only be achieved by coordination with the man on the rudder, who would have to turn the barge in order to fire in any direction besides straight ahead.

On the side of the right-hand board he fixed the lever-released crank shaft, inserting its axel through the hole intended for it, and then the wooden pins that would hold it in place, securing them with large nails. Between the boards he set the open steel spring tube, nailing its lip to the ledges of the boards in four places on either side, then looping the strong rope cord around the hook on the spring, fixing it to the axel of the crank and winding the slack out. He inserted the crossbar through its holes in the boards, which set it just below the spring tube, hammering the plates which held it fast. Then he strang the thick, flexible strap composed of banded cow intestines around the hooks on either end of the crossbar, pulling them back to the hook on the spring at the bottom of the tube where the rope cord connected to the lever-released crank shaft. Finally he worked a liberal amount of grease over the mechanics, layering the open steel spring tube with it, the axel of the crank shaft, and the rope wound round it.

In the meantime, he had the Nubians and the mercenaries constructing shields at staged points on the sides of the barge using the extra planks from the docks and by ripping up some of the boards from the deck, which in turn provided stations that lowered their silhouette while they rowed from the spaces between. He stopped only once to stand and eat a few handfuls of tough, salt-dried meat that made his gums bleed. By the end of the humid, overcast day he had sweat through his robes several times over, and sat in his loincloth and head dress with his back to one of the palm trees drinking an amphora full of water, holding it in his filthy, grease-blackened hands and bringing it to his lips from which it ran down his chin and throat and etched canals through the grime layering his chest and torso. He'd forgotten to shave.

In the coming days they moved out of Babylonia into the most ancient region of Mesopotamia, the land of the Sumerians, of writing and the wheel; an area of primeval urbanization around ziggurat temples built as gateways to the gods or, as legend had it, in remembrance of the mythical mountains the mysterious people originally migrated from. In any event, their once-green fields, where peasants with scythes had happily harvested the fruits, olives, vegetables, dates and grain for their beer, were all desert now, the irrigation canals that fed them buried under thousands of years of time, and echoed only by isolated pockets of mosquito-infested marsh. Just as iron turned to rust, Lucullus reflected, all the proud men turn to dust.

In the late afternoon of the third day, however, when Uruk began to grow on the horizon, the trapper realized that he too was going to die. The sound of screaming greeted them before the city did, a vast, sand-blasted ruin five or six miles inland from the Euphrates framing a weathered nub of once-huge ziggurat. But the Parthian toll station which grew out of the old Seleucid commercial city of Orchoi bordering the river, replete with its boat bridge and toll booth to regulate traffic, was still intact. And, sure enough, a platoon of Sassanid horsemen were loping back and forth along the quays, herding Sand People and tribal squatters into forced conscription for the coming war against Rome; as well as torturing the Mediterranean merchants and tradesmen who, like Batiatus, had been caught short in the fall-out.

Options raced through Lucullus' mind. They were blocked by the boat bridge with its toll booth. He could abandon the barge and try to escape due west over five hundred miles of desert to Petra and die of thirst, walk east into Persia and die many different ways, or turn back north to Babylon and probably die as well. But then he recalled a line of Arrian in reference to Alexander, whose ghost had haunted him along the entire way . . . 'Nothing put him off. Starvation, the freezing cold, nothing – he just kept coming on and on. And in the end his enemies were struck with fear and amazement.'

So he slung his father's sword and his silver-plated gorytos crossways around his torso and he took his fine Scythian bow and walked calmly to the front of the barge and began filling the cauldrons with the amphorae full of flammable oil that he'd purchased from the quartermaster at Babylon. He lit a handful of embers from a small lamp and the three cauldrons of Greek Fire leapt into flames at their touch. With his signal, the Nubians immediately mounted their hide shields across the rowing spaces between the wood-plank battlemounts, then took back up their oars under cover of the shields. The barge now trailed three coils of oily black smoke from the cauldrons at its prow.

Batiatus was wringing his hands and trying to put on a brave face, nodding, "Come on now, lads. That's it." He turned to Lucullus, "What the devil are we going to do?"

Loading the first bolt into the open steel spring tube of his homemade ballista, the striations in the trapper's forearms writhed in the sunlight as he wrenched the lever-released crank shaft tightening the rope cord that pulled the strong strap of banded cow intestines. "Well, I'll tell you one thing we're not going to do," he replied, as the bolt shifted ominously down into the spring-coiled depths of the tube, " is pay the toll." He looked up at the little fat man and shook his head, "On this river, anyway. Maybe to Charon on the Styx in a few minutes," he smiled.

Batiatus smiled back cheerily and wiped the sweat from his brow.

"Tell your men to pick up speed on the rowing," Lucullus yelled at the mercenary captain. "Then, at my command, every other man shift to cover fire with his bow." Turning to Batiatus, "I need you on the rudder," he nodded. "I may need you to turn the barge to help me fire this," he cocked his head at his homemade ballista. "But mostly keep it straight on. We're going to bash through."

"Right," blinked the wide-eyed, fat little merchant, bringing his fist to his chest in salute.

The mercenaries had half-heartedly taken up positions with their bows, but they were

101

acting quirky and indecisive, lingering too far back and not rowing. With the icy remembrance of the kicking of their captain and his decision to keep the Syrians in front of him, or his Nubians behind them, at all times, the trapper spoke calmly to the little fat man, "And keep an eye on them will you," he nodded in indication of the mercenaries as he began to work with the elevation stem on his rather shaky ballista.

Batiatus' jowls trembled and he blinked his bulging eyes, but his upper lip remained stiff. "Right."

The first of the quays was still a hundred yards off when the Sassanid spotted them and reined up his fine stallion broken wild off the Bactrian steppes. His horse stamped sideways and whickered. The rider was tall and handsome, and wore makeup and earrings, the eye maskara serving the dual purpose of ennobling him and cutting the desert glare. He wore the armor of his grandfather, who had fought for the Parthians against the legions of Marcus Aurelius – a gold-banded silver skull cap from the back of which his oiled black hair fell in a mass, a thick-woven golden vest embroidered in chrysanthemum design over his long-sleeved tunic of ringlet mail, and segmental leg armor that flexed at the joins. At his alert, more than twenty of his men broke from their devastation and began loping down the river bank toward the barge in an undulating line of silver and gold flashing in the sunlight.

Flames roiled from the hellenistic porticos lining the docks. Some of the merchants and tradesmen were nailed to the wooden doors of the warehouses, their guts spilling out, screaming to death. Others were being forced to their knees and beheaded while their women were raped in alleys.

As the line of horsemen came level with the barge, their leader called out to them in Persian, and then Aramaic.

"This is what we're paying you for," the trapper nodded at the mercenary captain. "Tell him what he wants to hear, but keep your men rowing." He shook his head. "We're not stopping."

The captain answered the Persian. An exchange of words followed in which Lucullus was perceptive of an atmospheric shift. The Persian's bearing was demanding; the Syrian's deferential. He looked around at his men and the Nubians, while the Persian kept pointing at the boat bridge. The mercenary captain then turned back to the Persian and nodded, and began speaking Syriac in low tones to his men, who were nocking arrows onto their bows.

Batiatus barely had time to yell, "Mutiny!" when Lucullus sprang out of a crouch at the captain, covering the ten feet between in a second. One of his Nubians took an arrow for him as he plunged his fat Spanish-style dagger through the Syrian's sternum and another of his blacks fell and the rest began slashing and dancing with their spears. Knocked down by the body of the Nubian who cheated death for him, another of the mercenaries leapt toward the trapper sword-raised, but Batiatus scurried like a spider across the deck and hamstrung him with his letter-knife. The mercenary fell hard onto the planks screaming and trying to bring his sword into the little fat man but the trapper rolled to an elbow, drew his own blade over his back and smashed downwards severing the Syrian's arm. A fan of bloodspray shot across the planks.

Lucullus immediately rolled to the side and up, and then plunged his sword into the screaming Syrian, silencing him. He cast a quick glance at Batiatus, who looked at his letter-knife and shrugged, and then felt something tug hard on his flowing robe before realizing that a Persian arrow had ripped through it and sunk into the deck with the others starting to hammer into the planks and shields around the ledge of the barge and zip through the spaces between. The last of the mercenaries were being outmaneuvered by the superior athleticism of the Nubians, one of whom arced and collapsed wide-eyed onto the deck with the quill of an arrow protruding from his shoulder blades.

Lucullus crawled rapidly back to the ballista and lit the oil-soaked chunk of palm trunk in the incendiary housing of its bolt. "Stay tight to the shields!" he yelled at Batiatus, for the Persians were now expertly arcing their arrows into the deck of the slow-floating target, "and get to the rudder!"

Blood rolled in sun-glinting rivulets over the deck, and another Nubian took an arrow in the skull as he struggled with the last of the mercenaries. Lucullus grabbed his Scythian bow and, from a knee, put an arrow through the mercenary while the rest of the blacks leapt back to their oars and began rowing hard. The ones on the Persian side of the bank were shielded, but the others vulnerable to arcing arrows. The trapper motioned for every other man on the shielded side to return fire.

The boat bridge was a hundred yards out, low fishing skiffs tied together with platforms established across them and a small wooden booth-structure in the central section where the toll officials had taken their fees in more lawful days. His stomach and back muscles drawn taut, aiming for the bridge at the base of the booth, the trapper threw the lever back on the crank shaft and watched helpless as the flaming bolt shot two feet over the bridge and dove into a harmless hiss in the river.

He rolled frantically to grab another bolt. The Persians were galloping for the floating bridge and reining in their horses to start across it. Slamming the next steel javelin in place and holding the lamp to the sack-filled mix of palm nuts and oil-soaked rags filling its incendiary housing, he popped the boards of the ballista into a higher notch on the elevation stem, cranked wildly at the shaft until it was at maximum tension, and threw the lever back again. The bolt blasted into the base of the toll booth, igniting it; but the bridge did not break.

"Turn me to the left!" he screamed at Batiatus, loading a third bolt into the spring tube and cranking as fast as he could while the barge's prow began to drift left. He threw the lever back and the bolt rocketed into the boat bridge halfway between the shore and the toll house. Three horseman skidded and plummeted into large wave-throwing splashes in the river. The horses behind balked at the fire licking across the platform, and two more riders were thrown.

Turbo took an arrow through the outside of his buttock while setting a fourth bolt. Grinning with the pain, he loaded two of the slender amphorae full of flammable oil in the bolt's incendiary housing and then cranked it back. With a roar, he sent the bolt racing into the flaming boats halfway between the shore and the toll house, where the amphorae in its incendiary housing shattered and erupted on the extant flame in a great gout of angry red and black.

"Turn me back center!"

The section of the bridge near the shore broke away, but the center still held and his Nubians rowed toward it as the arrows rained down and another of them fell. Lucullus screamed in rage and took up his bow and began returning fast and accurate arrow fire, killing as many of the Persians' horses as he could. He had just enough time to drop the bow, load another bolt, and send it through the bridge at the base of the toll booth before the barge hit it and part of the booth collapsed across the deck in flames as the vessel scraped groaning across the sinking debris.

The trapper sprinted to the back and ripped up tents, unwilling to use their drinking water. Moving like a wild animal, he sprinted back to the front of the barge and used the tarps to smother the fire as best he could while the arrows continued to rain, but less now, because the river was wide enough and Batiatus astute enough to steer them as far away from the unfriendly shore as possible while the Nubians rowed like demons. Some of the Sand People and tribal conscripts were trying to escape, sprinting away, jumping in the river to swim toward the barge, whatever they could do. The fifty or so Persian horses had been lessened by ten or twelve, and the others were divided over trying to recapture the escapees with lassoes or gallop ahead and take up stations to try and bring Lucullus and crew down with arrows.

Their base was one hundred miles northeast at Susa, the current of the river swift, and by the time they came back in force, the barge would be long gone. Watching them hesitate, the trapper took up his bow, pulled an arrow out of the gorytos on his back, nocked it, drew back the string, elevated the bow and rocketed the arrow. The shaft whistled in an arc across the sky and then dropped into the chest of the Sassanid captain's horse, which screamed like a woman and spilled its rider in a golden-armored tumult of fallen pride.

The trapper raised his fist and screamed until the snot and saliva rippled from his mouth like wind-blown cobwebs. And then he stared the Persians out of sight, his face smoke-blackened and drawn, the back of his robe soaked with blood from his ass to his ankle. Three of his Nubians were gone, flames flickering on the railing of the barge, and Batiatus was nodding and shaking his head at the rudder. Gone indeed were the days under Trajan when the spice barges had passed each other daily on the Euphrates between Dura and the Gulf, and even the street whores in Rome could afford Indian perfume.

X

Lucullus and one of his Nubians dumped the bodies of the mercenaries overboard at the rear of the barge; an operation which painted their hands, arms and robes with sticky blood. The load of the craft lightened some, and he filled buckets with river water and threw them across the gore-painted planks of the deck. He brought water to each of his blacks, and indicated for them to rest at oars, for the current kept the barge moving well enough. Then he tended to the lifeless bodies of their three comrades, washing their death-wounds and covering them with the tarps that had not been scorched. They had paid the toll after all. And there wouldn't be any big game coming back up the caravan routes.

He threw the remnants of the toll booth which had collapsed onto the deck overboard. Batiatus finally made him stop for the blood that was slicking the rear of his robe. While it was still light, the little fat man used some of their drinking water to clean the gash across the side of the trapper's buttock where the arrow had furrowed it. Then he sewed it up with the needle and thread reserved for his sandals. Lucullus stared at the western horizon without making a sound or a face through the process. When finished, Batiatus applied a compress of myrrh from the trapper's kit to the wound, steadying it with a rag, which he then wound around him. "Good as new, old boy. Good as new, I say."

Lucullus distributed stale bread, goat cheese and cups of wine from an amphora to his Nubians, who sat at their oars, staring at the rose-colored bluffs passing by. For the lithe-muscled blacks, each sunset was a battle. In the north lived the one-armed warriors, the one-legged and one-eyed. They fought the sun each evening, spearing it to death until its blood ran out over the sky. But under the earth, in the night, the sun was born again, to come back each morning, new and the same.

The trapper watched them for a moment. Then he limped back to rear of the barge and poured wine for Batiatus and himself.

"Don't mind if I do," replied the little fat man, trying as always to remain cheerful.

The two men sat in silence on a trunk engraved with the letters S.P.Q.R., their backs to the rear ledge of the barge, Lucullus favoring his wound. He kept his hand on the rudder and watched darkness creep like an immense shroud over that ancient land of tyrant stargods with their lost methods and psychic gates for returning. The velvet blackness from the east purpled across the zenith overhead as it arced into the twilit blue, the last breath of day painting the atmosphere in gigantic shades of color which began blending softly into one another. They passed the buried mud-brick remnants of the primeval city of Larsa, then of Ur, where black-shadowed ziggurats broke the darkling horizon.

As the darkness progressed, the stars gathered above them like a river of milk across the sky, and Lucullus limped to the front of the barge and spoke with his Nubians. When he returned, he angled the craft over to the western river bank, the bank closest to their home, and threw anchor. The blacks disassembled the plank shields they'd constructed on the sides of the barge, prying them apart with their spears. Reverently handling their three lifeless comrades onto the ready-made funeral biers, they slipped overboard, bearing their dead as mystics who had discovered secrets they themselves would come to know. After a time, three distant bonfires lit the night with the ghostly figures of tall, sleek warriors wavering in their light.

Whether herded into service on the drives for game, or pressed into dock work loading cages, the tribesmen's birth-knots – the leather cords kept in their village shamans' sacred cow's liver bags – had all been untied for their dealings with the Romans. Untied, theirs were souls dead to the tribe, a mystery as potent as that of the elephant graveyard. Lucullus would often see them reach their slender fingers down and touch the knotless strips of leather they had subsequently fastened to their belts, wondering if theirs were, like his own, the type of minds that understood regret. And yet they had formed a tribe of their own, with the trapper as their chief, and he felt responsible for each one of them, in the same strange and painful way as he did for the lives of the animals he delivered to be slaughtered. For his Nubians, God was both Good and Bad, both Creator and Destroyer. Both Sun and Darkness, both Black and White. And Lucullus understood them.

He and Batiatus sat in silence on the barge as the warriors' soulful funeral dirge rent the night. Their primal cries strangely harmonized, and sent chills up their spines.

"Poor lads," said the little fat man after a time.

The trapper glanced at the bonfires, which burned bright, and then turned his face away, and gazed out into the vast eastern night. "Do you have any family?" he asked.

"Well," laughed the little merchant, "I suppose you could say so. I've a villa at Rome," he nodded. "My daughter lives there," smiling. "She won't speak to me. Hasn't in ten years. Won't answer my letters," he shrugged and looked up at the stars. One dropped off, and raced away from its brothers.

"I guess I had it all confused with duty," the little fat man continued. "Serving the state, providing for them. Couldn't get the hang of the balancing act," he chuckled. "If you get my drift, that is."

"I suppose I was away too much," he nodded. "We had . . . wonderful times, though," squinting his eyes. "Wonderful times," he smiled, and then raised his fuzzy grey eyebrows, and took a short breath, as if paying tribute to the fact that life never ceased in its little surprises. "My wife is married to a consul now."

Lucullus looked at him, sitting there with his chubby little hands on his knees, his bald pate shining in the reflection of the bonfires, his curly gray hair protruding from the sides. "Just the one child?" he asked.

"Oh no," Batiatus replied softly, looking up at him. "I have a son," he nodded, as if gently correcting him, as if he should know. As if everyone in the world should know. "Fine young fellow," his eyes wide with pride, "my lad," lifting his fat little fist in a gesture of hope, "He's my greatest joy," he smiled, his jowls faintly shaking.

"Where is he?"

"He died on the Rhine last autumn," the little fat man nodded, still smiling.

XI

Three days later they stood on the docks at Charax and stared at the brackish waters of the Persian Gulf. A gray, unfamiliar and strangely unwelcoming sea bathed in a haze of stillness and heat. The conduits at the frayed mouths of the Tigris and Euphrates had long silted over with deposits, and the old Seleucid ports of Little Alexandria and Little Antioch were marked only by the sunblanched hulks of derelict ships which lay half-buried in the fields of dry, cracked mud. These were the waters that Trajan had viewed, the sight of which made him walk a bit apart from his umbrella-clad entourage and sit down on the sand, overwhelmed by the realization of his age and the immensity of a world that Rome would never fully have. A dream-world that had worn away the youth of the great Alexander with malaria, dysentery, and a dozen battle wounds, along with his increasingly frequent alcoholic binges brought upon by the death of his beloved friend.

They did what they could to sell the barge at a little market-town called Apologus, between the mouth of the Euphrates and the port of Charax – an impoverished community of Gulf pearl divers who sold their lightweight goods to merchants of the camel caravans. But the people had neither use nor money for the barge, so they simply abandoned it, and walked across the sun-cracked graveyard of half-buried hulks to the port of Charax, where Lucullus spent most of the day negotiating passage on an Indian trader's barque. A smallish boat, a fifty foot coast-hopper shallow to the water and curving at prow and stern, it bore a single sail and a crew of funny little brown-skinned men in loincloths captained by a happy-lilting skipper who spoke a smattering of Greek and did a humble business with the princes of Characene Arabia.

Batiatus took an interest in the proceedings. The little fat man hopped and danced around the boat out of habit, his expert eye appraising its carrying capacity in a wink. Always seeking the bright side of things, he seemed to overlook the fact that they had absolutely nothing to ship. Nevertheless he tried touchingly to communicate with the captain, who laughed and nodded along with him, trying just as hard. The man's mutilated Greek was, like the ruined cities along the Euphrates and the mud-sunk docks at the Gulf, the hangover of a world that Alexander the Great had almost created.

But communicating with sea and river captains was old-hat for Batiatus, for as an official Navicularus, a shipper, he made his living from the supply of commodities throughout the world. Like Lucullus' grandfather, those of his guild were involved in supplying the legions stationed on the frontiers of the Empire, and their profit was made in using the surplus carrying capacity of the ships they hired to further their own interests. The State, which directed all mercantile and shipping activities, left them room for this.

And though Rome's contribution to Civilization – the standardized sensibility, the unified scheme of administration, the crystallization of mankind's social, political, artistic and technological advances and the re-application of them with a sensibility which took its cue from Greece – might be dated, Roman money was still money to the Indian trader, the mercantile world still lubricated by her dominant coin. So they set out the next morning, and kept to the Arabian side of the Gulf away from Persia. The flat-bottomed craft rode high on the water, and was ideally suited for the mussel shoals and shallows. They sailed past the myriad Calxi islands, which extended along the shore for a hundred miles or more, their inhabitants a treacherous lot whom the little Indian sailors were frightened of, for they infrequently preyed on the small-time traders and pearl divers, more out of spite than commerce. Several fishing skiffs came out at them one night with howls and spears, but it was little more than recreation for the Nubians, and a chance to try out the incendiary arrows, which, anyway, Lucullus wanted to conserve.

In the coming days, they made a stop at Gerrha, and then Omana, the white-stuccoed port cities of Arabic nomads coordinated by self-made princes who had enriched themselves on the caravan trade. Their harbors were lined with madarata, the sewn-together cane boats, as well as larger vessels from India and Persia that came to trade in wine, dates, slaves and gold. Large deposits of copper, sandalwood, teakwood, blackwood and ebony filled the docks, and the scent of frankincense mingled with the salt-sea air. The captain of the Indian trader sold spice, unguents, pepper and perfume to the Arab merchants, who would in turn send them across the caravan routes to Petra. And then up the Via Traiana, Trajan's highway to the Mediterranean port of Tyre, where they would be sold to Roman Negotiatores for a great profit that, as a consequence, would limit their availability to only the very rich in the capital.

When they left Omana, they turned northeastwards along the great sharp promontory that nearly closed the Gulf and turned it into a salt lake, rounding its tip past the large island of Sarapis flanking the opposite shore. They made a stop on the island to barter with its settlement of Fish-Eaters, who spoke a version of the Arabian language and wore girdles of palm-leaves. The Indian captain traded pearls for the fine-quality tortoise-shell which the island produced in considerable quantity, and for which small sailboats and cargo-ships were sent regularly from Cana and Moscha on the Arabian peninsula.

The moon grew slender and then fat again and, when Lucullus wasn't playing at knucklebones with Batiatus over their evening wine, he read Homer or himself composed a few fairly competent lines. The trapper's verses reflected on man's greatest duty which, as he saw it, was to fight his fate, and give it no quarter; to strive to blot out his written doom, and to surpass his god. But mainly he turned his mind to the task at hand. For though he'd had good intentions upon his return to the Claudianus Mons with his diploma, intentions to present it to his parents as a gift along with his decision to forsake his weird longings and live a life of the mind, of the intellect – intentions to accept the assistant professorship offered him at the Mouseion – the smell had hit him before the sight of the place.

When he'd rounded the hillock into the wadi, the legionaries were burning the bodies in mass graves and spreading the trenches with lime. A fever had swept the camp and his parents had both died. He burned them separately and his diploma with them, and he placed the ashes in a finely crafted urn decorated with a motif of Achilles and Ajax shooting dice, which he then buried in the foundations of the Capitolium. He viewed the body of the green-eyed whore whom he still loved, and he knew that the halls of his memory would long echo her lies. And then he walked out of the wadi and he never looked back.

He was soon enough with a crew of trappers learning things like how to dig just the right pit, surround it with a wooden fence, and tether a calf inside. When anything ranging from a leopard to a lion heard the calf bleating, it jumped over the fence, and the weight of the fall plunged it into the pit. He took place on massed hunts, running and shouting with the blacks driving herds of antelope into rivers where they were lassoed by men waiting in boats, or down ravines covered with slippery rawhides so that the animals lost their footing and were hogtied by the men below. He was often one of the hundreds of beaters that moved in from all sides through a stretch of jungle, driving the animals into a circle where Numidian spearmen with oval shields formed a wall around the captive beasts and held them long enough for others with lassoes and nets to complete the job.

Through the years, his body grew as hard and unforgiving as his mind, and his strange and displaced childhood gave him a ruthlessness which was essential to his chosen profession. His connections with the barge men on the river gave him an edge as well, and he worked his way up in the business until he had his own contingent of loyal Nubian hunters. Together they caught elephants by driving them into box canyons, and then used trained elephants to lead them out. They caught chimpanzees and baboons by putting out big bowls of wine and then picking up the animals after they were drunk. His Nubians caught pythons by placing long bags of rushes near the snakes, then agitating them. The serpents slithered into the bags thinking they were holes, and the blacks pulled the cords that closed them.

Lucullus' techniques were as ingenious as they were endless. He would use oryx for bait, letting a lion, leopard or a cheetah catch one, and while it was feeding, have his Nubians sneak up and net the beast. For the loading process onto galleys, the trapper used British fighting dogs, which he'd trained to snap along at the flanks of rhinos and elephants as they were pulled aboard with ropes.

They skirted the Gedrosian coast and made a short stop in the run-down port of Pasni, and then in the larger one of Barbaricon, where the great Indus river split into seven mouths, its enormous volume turning the ocean fresh and causing great serpents to come forth from its depths and roil round passing ships. The little loin-clothed crew speared a few of the eels and roasted them on the deck for dinner as they anchored off the small island in the bay. They drank sweet Arab wine and Batiatus smacked his lips. "Nice change from the same old fish, I'm sure."

The next morning, the Indians traded topaz, coral and frankincense for bdellium, turquoise, silk yarn and indigo while Lucullus, Batiatus and the Nubians stayed aboard. For the port town was technically a Parthian holding and, though the signs of upheaval had not yet reached it, there was no sense in taking chances. They set off that evening under towers of golden cumulus cloud for the two hundred-mile trip around the promontory enclosing the Gulf of Baraca. The crew kept their craft well out to sea to avoid its shifting sandbanks, sharp shoals, eddies and whirlpools. Two days later they turned inward along the southern side of the promontory toward the Bay of Barygaza – mouth of the Narmada River, Port of the Malwa Raj, and gateway to all of India.

For two hundred years, Roman Navicularii had bought wheat, rice, sesame oil, clarified butter and cotton there. They'd also procured precious stones, onyx and sardonyx, diamonds and sapphires. From their capital at Minnagara, upriver from Baygaza, the Malwa Rajahs controlled the carnelian and agate industry of western India, mined from the abandoned courses of the Narmada which, over the eons, had washed them out of the volcanic basalt through which it flowed.

In the immediate vicinity, however, in the mist-shrouded mountains of the Satapura Range, lay the industry in which Lucullus traded. For beyond the Port of Barygaza, the inland was rich in leopards, tigers, elephants, enormous serpents, baboons and hyenas, as far as the river Ganges. He saw several of the huge three-leveled monsoon vessels anchored in the bay, waiting for the winter winds that blew east toward Africa; and he felt the quickening of expectation while standing at the prow, breathing the closing smell of gray weather as the barque slid into the tree-clad mouth of the river, past its blue-and-gold-tiled shrines with their pointed domes, and a small derelict temple of Augustus and Rome. Constructed two centuries before by the first Latin traders in these parts, the handsome little structure sprouted flowering vines from cracks in its marble.

XII

They spent the first week resting, and in negotiations with the Raj. A pleasant little black-bearded man in an oversized turban, Lucullus had dealt with him before. And with his father, the late Raj, a man with mystic tendencies still preserved in the reign of his son by the brahmins who sat cross-legged at court. But the son was an epicure, and though he charged a bit more than Lucullus wanted to pay for the rhino, elephant and antelopes he had in stock, he promised a rich banquet at the end of the expedition along with the choice pick of his concubines, and of his singing boys, when the trapper returned.

At the start of the second week they left Minnagara, and set off across the dried gray bitter lakes that painted their calves with white chalk. Batiatus insisted on coming along and, as long as he had enough water, the little fat man proved surprisingly capable on the march. Lucullus fitted him out in the heavy Indian cotton trousers, the leather boots and long-sleeved tunic such as he himself wore, and the shipper had acquired a ridiculous, broad-brimmed hat dripping with tassels which he used to keep the sun off. Cheerful in all weathers, he never shirked a task, and Lucullus had taken a rare liking to him.

Each morning, after their breakfast of rice porridge, mangoes, and black tea flavored with cardamon, Lucullus would sling his gorytos, his Scythian bow, and his leather cup harness full of light javelins, and Batiatus would take up the absurd hunting spear that was over twice his height and which he'd gotten the gods knew where but insisted on carrying.

"Here we are," he would say. "Better to have this and not need it, than to need it and not have it, I'm sure."

And so they would set off, the Nubians flanking several hundred yards out on both sides, the three hundred Indian porters and the train of elephants bearing the supplies, the nets and the disassembled caging that, when filled, would have to be taken back down from the mountains and loaded onto the transport carts.

By the third week they were well beyond the lakes and had made the foot of the mountains, where they established a base camp and a station for the carts that would transport their catch back to the holding pens at the port. That evening they celebrated by feasting on gazelle, which Lucullus killed with expert bow shots. In the night, amidst his dreams, the trapper heard the cough of a leopard that had come for the leftover meat.

The next morning he awoke beneath a tremendous banyan tree, the sky spreading above him a light lime through its branches. The banyan trees reminded him of the fifty-foot monoliths quarried and fashioned at the

Claudianus Mons when he was a boy, though some were much larger. Their trunks had the same grayish color, with a faint yellow sheen. There were giant fig trees interspersed among them, and baboons had been eating their fruit. The cool of the morning brought out the smell of their droppings, which mingled with the rotting smell of the burst figs littering the ground.

The Hindi porters were cooking the rice porridge for breakfast. The Nubians sat in a circle. The leopard that coughed in the night was hanging placidly in a net from the branch of a tree at the edge of the grove, to be carted to the river by the porters and sent back to Minnagara with the rest of their growing catch. The trapper was pleased with the expedition thus far. The animals had come in nicely, gazelle from the herds that wavered across the prehistoric lakes, antelope his Nubians had caught in the ravines.

When they made the mountain country, they found it inhabited by numerous tribes, all more or less subject to the Raj. Lucullus saw ancient Greek drachmae being used among them, along with fragments of inscriptions in provincial Greek lettering hanging over an old village mystic's shack. Some of the guides he hired from the villages pointed out to him relics in the hills which they said were from the expedition of the Great Iskander – ancient shrines, ruined walls, remnants of wells. But it was the beast that roamed in solitude through the high, volcanic lake country that the trapper sought.

So he moved into the forest-clad hills, using the elephant trails that formed perfect roads through the overgrowth, the trees bordering them worn smooth by the flanks of the wise old beasts. Other trails intersected them haphazardly like city streets. The light was beautiful, deep and full of shadows, and penetrated in places by thrusting sunbeams. It reminded Lucullus of certain abstruse pieces of music he'd heard while at the Mouseion, and he recalled that this was the country where Dionysus was said to have been born, the god of wine and revelry, of joy in action, ecstatic motion and inspiration. The god of instinct and adventure and dauntless suffering; the god of music and dance and song.

Then came the weeks which he passed in the shelters they built in the trees at various points throughout the hills and for the duration of which he did not speak but simply waited and watched, often staring for an entire day at the large red and green caterpillars that inched infinitely over the thick gray branches while he felt that familiar ferment in his soul that would be destroyed by dilution the next time he spoke a Greek or Latin word. He stayed up in the tree-houses until he became part of the forest itself, and felt his own life-force to be simply a version of that which moved in the dark, patient torpidity of the plant kingdom. But then he would hear the far-off clopping sound made by the hollow blocks of wood that one of his Nubians was signaling with a hundred yards away, and he would feel the adrenaline start as one of the great striped cats wandered panting through the forest floor below toward the smell of the fresh antelope carcass he had placed at the base of the tree.

When he dropped the stone-weighted nets down upon them, the tigers' struggles indelibly entangled them. Once they were tired enough, and never without some buried sense of regret, Lucullus would lower himself on the strong vine ropes while the porters moved in upon the beast with their opium-laced blow-darts to inflict the superficial wounds that were yet enough to subdue the animal while they caged it. From the ground he would wait behind the netting they had spread over vast swathes of uneven, tree-clad territory while the hundreds of porters moved in from opposite sides blowing conch horns, banging cymbals and uttering cries. He watched in somber awe as the cats raged against the nets, blasting into trees, tearing down saplings, rolling and fighting as the porters closed in with the blow-darts that each time he almost did not let them shoot but for the fact that the world must be ruled not by love alone but by the more ruthless principles of what is most needed.

He stalked the colonies of wild mountain pigs and wonderfully spotted deer, crouching in the treelines bordering the cool, mist-shrouded surfaces of black water where they drank, his legs double-wrapped with hide against the snakebites that had already killed six of the

Indian porters, situating his body and trying to keep his gorytos, bow, and the harness of javelins on his back from rattling. The Nubians moved like ghosts to either side of him in an arc about the ponds where they took up positions, and he watched the pigs wade out into the water, snuffling and slurping, rooting and pushing each other out of the way, nudging with their little tusks. The groups of wonderfully spotted deer clopped warily toward the surface of the pond spreading, like the sky, with a soft gauze of lemon that was still mostly absorbed by the deep blue-black behind it.

The air was heavy and still, and strangely devoid of the sudden freshening it usually underwent before the sunrise, no matter where in the world he happened to be, and especially in the high country. Diana, goddess of the hunt, felt close, and there was no need to consider the direction of the wind. Steam billowed noiselessly from his mouth as he forced himself to listen more carefully despite the inturning of his effort, his eyes glancing off tree trunks further into things that might mean something, might not.

And then one of the deer on the opposite shore would raise its head and Lucullus would feel an atmospheric shift as the tiger exploded from the reeds, covering forty yards from a stand-still in three seconds, the herd of deer turning as one and then fragmenting into the desperate hop-jumps that enabled most of them to escape, save the destined one which the cat sank with and then began slowly and clumsily swimming back to the shore line with, the deer's eyes moist and wide and lost in shock, the trapper rising and jogging forward opening his net, the pigs scurrying off squealing through the undergrowth beneath the trees, the tiger dropping the deer and lunging toward the bank, the Nubians moving low out of the reeds. And then the blacks casting their own nets and the turmoil in the reeds, the violence not at all with the kingly dignity of the lion nor of any other open-field cat but Dionysiac, insane in its razor-sharp soul of pure crystalline individuality.

Batiatus stayed in the centrally-localized village where they headquartered, bartering for interesting stones or old Greek coins, walking about in his ridiculous, tassel-draped hat and followed in train by naked children, bare-breasted women and shaggy-haired men all full of yellow-toothed laughter. But the cages were coming down from the mountains and, after three months, Lucullus estimated that, with the elephants and rhino purchased from the stock of the Raj, their catch of antelope, gazelle, leopards, baboons and pythons was enough to turn a profit in Rome after shipping costs. And the thirty-nine tigers contained a good mix of males and females for his breeding purposes.

Thirty-nine tigers but the trapper wanted a fortieth, and he waited all of one night on the rim of a small volcanic crater lake. It was nearly dawn, and through a parting in the shadowy western ridges he could see the dry lakes and the river Narmada beyond – a black squiggle moving at an oblique angle toward the coast. A faint twinkling marked the lights of Minnagara and, farther on, barely perceptible save for his fine eyesight, those of the port of Barygaza.

A tiger came to the watering hole to drink. A rogue, like all of his temperament from any species, living in solitude in country high above the others. It raised its head and sniffed the air and hissed wildly at the man-smell. Its green eyes sparkling, its face assumed one of the most godlike expressions that danger ever could. The sun broke blindingly and turned the surface of the water into a golden mirror, and Lucullus realized that Apollo, the god of clarity and intellectual contemplation, of logical order and philosophical calm, the god of painting and sculpture and epic poetry, had met Dionysus. He motioned to his blacks to leave the cat alone, for he had never begun a day with more grandeur.

Back in Minnagara, the banquet was as promised. The cattle roasted on spits, and the languorous, smooth-bellied women danced to the music of the long-eyelashed pages. The confusion of acrobats and dancers, the dishes laden with exotic viands, the bacchanalic revelry and the superfluous beauties – all of it seemed unclean after the hard purity of the mountains, where life and death were uncluttered and immediate. Still, Lucullus was not one to disdain others' pleasures, like the token brahmins who sat cross-legged and hollow-eyed, unmoved by the tastes, sounds and colors. For he knew that to play the philosopher amidst epicures was also a form of self-indulgence.

So he reclined on the mountains of huge feather pillows in a light robe embroidered in Indian design and open at the chest, his hands behind his head, his legs stretched out and crossed. Batiatus sat near him with a haunch of beef in his hand, licking the grease off his fingers before starting in on the dessert of monkey brains spooned direct from their open craniums. And the trapper smiled, content with his catch as he watched the pearls tremble on the belly of a dancer he came to fancy.

That night he lay on a carpet of wool on the floor of a room hung with gleaming brocades while a brown-skinned girl with eyes like a panther massaged his feet. The encounters in the mountains spun through his head – the morning mists, the nets, the pythons wrapped round the banyan branches and the storm of orange, black and white in the reeds. From the ornate, iron-lanterned corridors of the palace and through its elaborately-screened causeways came the sounds of the Indian night – the whispering of slaves, the soft rustle of palms, the layered sounds of the citharas and the melancholy murmur of a song.

XIII

They passed a pleasurable month in the palace of the Malwa Raj, where Lucullus tried not to get used to the dancer whose pearls trembled on her belly. The Raj made a present of her to him, but he had no use for her other than the one, and that wasn't enough. Then it was time, the monsoon had arrived, and the docks at Barygaza were cluttered with commerce – huge bales of cotton en route to the clothiers at Alexandria, silk cloth, mallow cloth, yarn, spikenard, costus, bdellium, ivory, agate and carnelian.

The day lay blanketed under heavy cloud, and the smell of aromatic ointments rode heavy on the dank morning air. The sounds of gold and silver coins tinkled through the mismatch of languages and the shouts of the dockworkers. Transport ships from Moscha, Cana and Muza on the Arabian peninsula prepared for their return, as did the large vessels bound for Opone and the Spice Cape of East Africa. Lucullus had purchased space on three of the large monsoon vessels for the several hundred antelope and gazelle, the fifty or more leopards, twenty baboons, thirty-nine tigers, twenty-four rhino and the eighteen elephants that were being led over the iron and log planks into the cargo holds. If not for the revolution in Mesopotamia, he could have procured three times the amount of beasts and sent two-thirds of them up the caravan routes to be relayed to Rome from the holding stations at Tyre and Sidon.

He watched the lines of Bactrian galley slaves being taken up the planks and chained to the two floors of oars in each of the ships. Behind him, the long-stretching wagon train of animals moved slowly in, the smell of the beasts pungent over the vats of spices, perfumes and unguents all destined, as well, for Rome. The loading process had begun the day before, and was almost complete. He'd taken pains over the animals, making sure that their cages were as well-spaced as possible, their food and water supplies regulated and secure, moving between the ships with his Nubians while Batiatus ran up and down the docks buying up as much as he could of the silk cloths, spices, perfumes and rare stones that Lucullus had loaned him money for.

The trapper was below decks when they departed, carefully drugging the animals through their water with the opium he had bought in large quantities at the dark offices of a Chinese merchant on the docks. The cargo holds were below the floors of oars, poorly ventilated and full of the smell of the wilds. In the evening, when he had finished, he climbed thankfully to the deck of the large ship, ate raw oysters, drank yellow wine and watched the stars mount one by one to the sky.

The moon had filled again, and he gazed at it as it rose and fell with the horizon, huge and mystic and golden. Like the wife he'd never married, and could never stay faithful too, the goddess Luna reminded him of his follies; for her phases, like that of a woman's, had always provided the feel of the passage of time for him moreso than calendar days. But there was always that great whore Cybele, goddess of Earth, who pulled at his heart strings as well; who filled him with the Siren song and the thirst for distant shores, shores where the sky kissed the sea and he touched the golden beaches with tears of brave Ulysses.

The experience of travel had served to deepen his curiosity for the world, and feed his lust for living. The taverns of Alexandria, the brothels of Sardis, and all the great drives for game. While a student he'd developed an interest in the ancient and obscure cults which claimed to have some key to the mysteries of the Earth, for their strident music appealed at that moment in his life when dance left him reeling, and song ended in outcry. He subsequently sought out the orgies of Cybele, the Thracian feasts of Orpheus, and the gliding of the milk-fed serpents at the Cave of Trophonius.

For a time he thought he had heard harmonies osmotizing out of life's discords. But he was younger then, and since realized that a man had to find his own way to gaze upon the abyss without the disintegration of his soul – to gaze upon it with heroic and playful eyes, devoid of fear yet also of hope. And to be filled with coherence, pride and manliness by a vision.

The wind was right, and the three-masted monsoon ships made the Spice Cape in eleven days, where the Berber dockmen awaited their season of work. Lucullus lost one of the rhino to the journey but, other than that, was pleased with the survival rate. The offloading of the animals was complicated by the traffic jams created by other ships arriving daily, and they worked long days supervising the transferral of the beasts to the vast stockyards where they were able to rest and exercise for the week it took him to contract the myriad smaller vessels that would transport them up the Red Sea. There were the usual escapes from mishandled caging that resulted in several deaths among the slaves, but he knew all of the Negotiatores at the port, and Batiatus was of use as well; together they were able to press the contractual arrangements through with some celerity.

When all was arranged, Lucullus, Batiatus and the Nubians set out on the first of the ships with the tigers, for the cats did not do well on the journeys, and their survival necessitated a precision of food, water, and opium. They made a stop in the port town of Avalites, where they drank the sour grape liquor from Diospolis in a tavern full of rank-smelling sullen Berbers while the rain rippled across the bay. And then at Adulis, where Lucullus could remember elephants and rhino being trapped right up to the coast in other days, but which were now at best a week's journey inland along with the tribes that used to attack merchant vessels, but which had likewise been pushed further back by the slave trade.

Then there was the large port of Berenice, where the Via Hadriana began, the highway that ran the two hundred miles up the coast to the Claudianus Mons, the Porphyrites Mons, and then due east to the Nile. The Latin tongue had become more prevalent, and the trapper was now using it instead of Greek to deal with ship captains and shopkeepers. He picked up a few new tunics, and a hooded military paenula, for it was the month of Tybi, and the Mediterranean would be cool. Batiatus purchased a set of cups and a pitcher made from rhinoceros horn for his daughter who wouldn't talk to him; and then they continued north by sea, passing the Smaragdus Mons and the small ports at Nechesia, Leucos Limen, and Philotera, before stopping at the harbor of Myus Hormus.

Batiatus was proving ever-more capable in this part of the world, and the Nubians had developed a strange appreciation for him. For anyone as ridiculous as the little fat man was either a wizard or a demon in their minds. The shipper spoke to them just as he did to Lucullus, and just as if they understood every word that he said when they understood absolutely none of it. They watched him with blank expressions as he performed magic tricks on the deck of the ships at night, with trinkets, eggs and string; and they sat in a circle and cocked their heads while he told them fanciful tales, his eyes bugging, his jowls shaking with enthusiasm.

Lucullus left the assembly of the camel caravan to him, and he rented a horse and rode the fifty miles south to the Claudianus Mons, where he rounded the hillock into the wadi and faced the beauty and the pain of his return. The last major production of the quarry had been for the Baths of Caracalla in Rome, completed ten years prior, for which it produced the fifty-foot monoliths that upheld the vault of the frigidarium, and the hundreds of others necessary to a Roman architectural complex enclosing an area of fifty acres. Otherwise, the place did not work on the scale that it once had.

He climbed the cracked sandy steps of the Capitolium and revered the grave of his parents, burning incense on the plaque in the floor in the cool shadows of the temple. Then he went down into the quarries, and walked in silence among the thousands of derelict columns that were the same ones he'd played amongst as a child. He climbed atop the two-hundred ton 'mother' and sat and watched the sunset with melancholy nostalgia, and then spent the evening as the guest of the current commandant, who lived with his wife and two children in the same house on the hill in which Lucullus had grown up.

The next morning he returned to Myus Hormus to find Batiatus astride a camel with his ridiculous tassel-draped hat on, all round belly and stout little legs sticking out from the sides of its hump.

"Ugly beast, I'm sure. Doesn't mind me, though. Birds of a feather, we are. Ho-ho, yes well."

One of the Nubians held the camel by the bridle with his spear in the other hand, and the trapper could only shake his head. But the little fat man had seen to everything, and the tigers were in shaded cages on flat-bed carts driven by the Arab lackeys he'd hired, one of them reserved for the growing cache of trade articles he was determined to make a fresh start with in Rome. And so they set out overland on the Via Hadriana and made the three hundred miles along the oases to Antinoopolis in two weeks.

Memorial to an emperor's bedside narcissus, its flavor wholly Greek after its founder's taste, the city had seen better days. Its continual peristyles were cracked and in need of restoration by funds continually diverted by the almost one hundred years of constant warfare in the Empire since its establishment. But, for the first time in months that felt like years, they had returned to the world of Rome. And it was with no small emotion that they passed beneath the gateway's triumphal arch. That evening, Batiatus and the trapper watched a comedy of Plautus, with a gourd of wine and a meal of cold roast chicken laid out on the marble seat of the open-air theater. The little fat man roared with laughter, Lucullus reclined and smiled, and the pallor of the sunset slipped warm rose off the sandstone divinities lining the horizon.

Then it was the Nile again, that river so filled with memories for the trapper, its peach-colored cliffs and ancient water temples upheld by squat sandstone columns that echoed the trunks of its palm trees. The barge was huge, and of the same model as those he had ridden as a boy. One evening, as he and his Nubians made the rounds with the drinking horns, Lucullus caught sight of their reflection thrown long across the gold-slivered water. For a minute he found himself staring again at his first sight of the fly-covered lions sliding by, panting and watching him through the bars.

They passed a night in the torch-lit taverns at Memphis, and then took the Canopic branch of the Nile into Alexandria. After a long day of paper-work, the tigers were turned over to the care of the Port Legatus on the docks, where gray waves crashed under a storm-geen sky, and the flames in the lantern of the lighthouse pulsed through the clouds blanketing the bay. The massive pillars of the Temple of Isis rose on a ridge-crest overlooking the city, and a Roman sentry paced its porch, his red cape whipping in the wind. Lucullus and Batiatus wound their way through the streets with the rain making loud splats across the dusty flagstones, the reed-mat shutters swaying and the lightning beginning to make its way in from the sea.

The university grounds were deserted, and they walked alone beneath a peristyle past a row of monumental sphinxes and cynocephelai, the sound of a dog barking echoing through the deserted squares. Near the famous library, Lucullus turned under a brick archway, its flaking stucco run with grime, and Batiatus followed him down a narrow alleyway, their sandals rasping over the wet stones. The trapper unhooked a ring of iron keys from his belt and unlocked the heavy wooden door of his house, entering a room of surprising space, its squat, groin-vaulted ceiling hovering high above.

The half-moon windows in each of the four groins pulsed with lightning, and the little fat man jumped at the white glimpses through the room of faces and monsters screaming in silence from the shadows. On a slab of sandstone tabletop, Lucullus chinked the flint and blew on the straw and lit an ember, moving around the room with it, lighting the oil lamps that dangled from various lengths of bronze chain. An arched labyrinth full of animals came slowly into view. Preserved through the ancient wizardry of Egyptian taxidermy, there were lions, leopards, cheetahs, and the heads of rhino and water buffalo mounted on the walls above the stacks of scrolls and rows of books filling the wooden trellises and reed cupboards.

"Fetch a pretty penny at auction, I'm sure," blinked Batiatus, as he looked about the room.

The little oil lamps flickered as the cool feel of the storm penetrated the large, vaulted space; and Lucullus lit a coal fire in the grate and produced a jug of blood-red Samos to warm their bones and end the long day.

The next morning was sunny and bright and rain-washed and fresh, the streets a patchwork of color winding through an atmosphere of crashing light and plunging shadow. The trapper squinted at the whiteness of the linen tunics and the painful blue in the sky, and he saw the black cassocks of the priests of Isis snaking like an alabaster serpent up the path to their temple on the hill. From the blinding sandstone of the squares to the sanguine glow under the tents in the bazaars, the color and movement was accompanied like a dance by a cacophony of tones – the strident noise of the sistra, the clattering of the galli, and the insistent strains of the oboe providing a chorus to the cries of hawkers and sellers, and the surf noise of voices. Through it all, Lucullus, Batiatus and the Nubians made their way back to the port, where the tremendous obelisk from the reign of Tutankhamen still lay on the docks, and the caged tigers were being loaded into the belly of the transport ship.

XIIII

The stars spread above him like a dusting of diamonds across the black velvet tablecloth of an Arab jeweler. His eyes followed the slow oscillation of the mast as it moved among them, swaying from the red eye of Taurus to the tears of the Pleiades, from Pegasus to the Swan. Sinking into the western horizon, Castor and Pollux, patron divinities of the city of Rome, gleamed faintly. If the wind and the weather held, he'd be there in the morning, make Ostia around sunrise.

The dark-wine sea rolled and planed in gentle swells of waves that occasionally bucked their spray across the side and wet his lips with the taste of salt-brine, the ship's prow rising and ducking, its wooden planks creaking peacefully with the drone of the surf as the vessel rode the calm night wind. Lucullus adjusted his back to a more comfortable position on the aft bulkhead where he sat with his legs stretched out in their leather trousers and crossed at the ankles of his boot sandals. Most of the crew were asleep, shadowed clumps under blankets scattered about, the slaves at oars below. Only the ship's pilate stood lonely at the wheel.

They'd made a stop to refit and replenish on Crete, at Lasea, where Lucullus offloaded the tigers into individual pens for rest and exercise, and let each feed on antelope. He spent a few pleasant days on that strange, wild island with its three thousand year-old cities and its Alpine gorges, that synthesis of Greece and the Orient. The trapper was never there without marveling at a lost race so close to his own heart. The island's dreadful earthquakes symbolized by the Bull-God, the ancient Cretans had transformed terror into an acrobatic game wherein man's virtue, in a direct contact with the beast, became tempered, and triumphed.

He walked alone through crumbling palace halls, and gazed with melancholy joy upon the faded frescos of those strong, lithe, charming bodies tempered in direct contact with the bull, over whom they leaped and tumbled in simple, certain and graceful movements. One in particular caught his eye, a fishing scene, youths in a barque with the fish below. Out of nowhere one of the fish took wing and leapt from the water in disregard of its nature. Casting it off, striving to break the bonds of its water-bound plight and to take flight – the trapper saw in it God; the force of God that was in him.

After departing Crete, they sailed north into the seas of Homer, where a powerful feeling gripped Lucullus as he breathed deeply the fresh swells of wet air. It had been a long while since he'd had the privilege of enjoying Greece, mother of Rome, and he stood at the prow and let himself be intoxicated by the Aegean in the mildness of an early spring, with diaphanous sheets of rain rippling across the green-apple sea, and a haze of morning sunlight bathing the myriad islands of the Cyclades. As they sailed into Phaleron Bay, past Cape Sounion and the Temple of Poseidon presiding in rock-cut glory from the hill, gulls from the mainland flew out to the ship and played about her mast and rigging.

They stopped at the harbor of Piraeus, where the merchant captain offloaded his cargo of Egyptian grain. The Nubians stayed with the tigers while Lucullus and Batiatus spent a day wandering through the mellow light of Athens, in friendly contact with bare marble, marveling at her subtle lucidity, her odors of warm honey, salt and resinous wine. The city was continuing on in a pensive grace under the protection of her daughter Rome, but the signs of decline were evident. And the trapper realized that, before Rome fully died, Athens would be no more.

But the Acropolis still shimmered in the sunshine, and they climbed its long flight of twisting steps hewn from the very limestone itself. Both had tears in their eyes as they rounded the corner through the propylaea to come face to face with the Temple of Athena, its delicate traceries of blue, red and golden fresco fading in the reliefs of its gable. Lucullus never visited the place without receiving a sublime realization of from where it was he sprung – from the only culture which had once and for all separated itself from the monstrous, the shapeless and inert; the only to have invented a definition of method, a system of politics, and a theory of beauty. He reflected on how Dionysus had come out of India, clad in multicolored silks, laden with bracelets and rings, his eyes maskaraed with black, his fingernails painted crimson. And then, as he proceeded into Greece, his adornments fell from him one by one until he stood naked on a hill at Eleusis, and the god of ecstatic and visionary drunkenness had turned into Apollo, the god of serene beauty.

That night they ate grilled lamb on an uncured pine table outside a tavern at the foot of the Acropolis. The cave of Pan loomed in shadow above, the god who supposedly allowed the Athenians to give vent to the Dyonisiac savagery which all men possess, when they needed it most at the battle of Marathon. In the morning they sailed out of the port of Piraeus, through noble Phaleron Bay between the Isles of Salamina and Egina, where the Persian fleet was lured and sunk six hundred years before, their ships on fire as far as the horizon, the smoke blackening the sky.

They made the Isthmus of Corinth that evening, and the ship rowed into the ancient Diolkos, where she was affixed to a massive mechanical system which, with much creaking and groaning of levers and pulleys, drug it onto a tremendous carriage of slip wheels. The signs of decay, disuse and neglect were evident, and much of the more extensive apparatus of the diolkos lay derelict and rotting in silted canals – particularly that for the bigger warships and troop transporters, though small merchant vessels such as theirs could still be accommodated through channels kept open by private entrepreneurs. Nero had wanted to cut a canal through the Isthmus of Corinth to facilitate rapid transport to and from Palestine, and Asia beyond. But that was two hundred years before and the project had long since been abandoned.

Great barnacled hulks rusted in the pinkly glowing dusk which bathed the cliffs surrounding the bay, and naked boys fished with nets in the tide. Lucullus, Batiatus and the Nubians roasted fish over coal fires with the boys' fathers, drank resinous the wine and ate bread sprinkled with sesame seeds. The simplicity of the meal had an almost sacramental quality, and after it was over the trapper explained the Nubian's concept of the sunset to the strong, simple Hellenic fisherman while Batiatus performed his magic tricks for their sons.

"To them, the sunset is a battle," Lucullus said. "In the north live the one-armed warriors, the one-legged and one-eyed. They fight the sun each evening, spear it to death until its blood runs out over the sky," he gestured across the bay at the last bloodstains on the western horizon. "But under the earth, in the night, the sun is born again, to come back each morning, new and the same."

Before sunrise, the ship on its huge wheel system was affixed to three long trains of oxen, which pulled it the day long over the broad, rutted gulley of the isthmus toward its opposite shore. The men walked beside it, feeling the difference of the land, alternately hard and supple like its people. The galley slaves were allowed a wondrous stretch of their legs, and the pleasure of the sun on their skin while they walked in a train of clanking shackles. Girls watched them from the hills while they picked grapes for their tart wine, and Lucullus was refreshed by their simplicity and provincial appeal – a long way from their over-contrived counterparts in Rome and Alexandria. As they neared the opposite shore, the men boarded the ship, climbing up rope ladders. The grade into the bay was still maintained precisely, and the massive wheel system was attached by ropes to great iron anchors on the land as it rolled slowly into the water until the ship floated buoyant and the cart was pulled out again.

Thus they rowed into the sun-glittering Bay of Corinth, the city's walls still riddled with the shot holes made by Sulla's catapults two and a half centuries before. The vessel cut the emerald sea between mainland Greece and the Peloponnesus, land of the Ancient Spartans, and Lucullus steeled his heart with hard maxims of how the proud knights of Lakadaemon had met the shock of Persia's mailed battalions; not a little moved by the loyal young squires who died by their sides, captivated by the vision of all the brave warriors lying naked in the sun. They sailed out of the mouth of the bay past Patra and Messalongi and between the wooded isles of

Zakinthos and Kefalonia, and made a short stop at Rhegium, on the boot tip of Italy.

Yesterday they'd made the Straits of Messina, and the sea had lost its peace. The Scylla and Charybdis of Odysseus, he never liked the passage. He'd tried to read the bit about it in a tattered, leather-bound copy of Homer he carried with him, but in the end felt obliged to stand by while his blacks vomited over the railing. But now the sea was calm and the wind was right and when they'd slid into the Bay of Naples at sunset, between the island of Capri and the horn where the ancient Greek acropolis at Sorrentum sat in stately ruin on the clifftop, he knew he was home. He'd stood at the prow and watched the sun drop like a molten coin into its slot in the saddle of Ischia, Vesuvius looming ominous and moody as always, ice-blue in the glowing dusk with the lights coming up in Naples around the bay.

The mariners sat over their evening meal, clustered around small oil braziers eating bowls of stew with chunks of fish, squid and octopus caught in the dredging nets and cut up by the cook, who stirred them into a thick sauce of garlic and onions with plenty of pepper. He took his bowl and ate with relish. Like the stews that sailors make when they land on some deserted shore, the meal had no equal for nourishing his wayward soul. Afterwards, he retreated to the aft bulkhead with a skin of wine, where he sat and drank and dozed, but then awoke, his nostrils flaring as he sniffed the salt-sea air, strengthened as it always was when night began to slip toward morning.

He pulled the hood of his paenula over his head and took another pull of the harsh Rhodian wine, seeking to open his mind to the peace of the sea, the elements of water and air in their most massive of forms. The wine's salt-water preservative quality made it a staple item of trade with India and the Orient, and he was reminded of moving in through a stretch of jungle with the copper-and-bile taste of fear in his mouth knowing that the beaters from the other three sides had just driven five hundred pounds of amoral lightning somewhere within a few feet of him.

He released the thought and looked behind him at the phosphorescent wake of the craft cutting back silver through the setting moon, adjusting his body to where he could better view that disk of glowing marble which had fascinated him since childhood. On the drives for game he would watch with wonder as it raced through the clouds of barbarian skies. Its light cast a sylvan glow over the deck of the ship, which was quiet save for its creaking, and the occasional guttural growl from below.

He'd kept the tigers doped for the passage. The opium concoction he purchased from that Chinese merchant worked its magic. Yet when they awoke, in Rome, they would awake angry.

Still, the cats were fine specimens. He checked on them personally a few hours before, their eyes mean and yellow and drugged, the iron cages packed tight and smelling horridly. With the opium it was important to make certain they were drinking enough water, and he'd made the rounds with the drinking horns several times a day.

When dawn broke, Lucullus still sat with his back to the aft bulkhead, the empty skin of salt-water Rhodian wine by his side. The Tyrrhenian Sea glittered in the morning sunlight, and he removed the hood of his paenula and let its warmth bathe his face. The great octagonal port of Ostia was coming into view on his right, vessels of all kinds crawling with the onset of a new workday, merchant ships of all races and peoples, from Spain to Palestine, shifting in the sunlit water by the docks. Out in the bay, more ships were arriving and departing, churning the water past the background spectacle of huge trireme transport ships, with three floors of a hundred oars each, docked off in the distance like blue hills. Above it all the deep blue arc of infinity reduced the massive port and its bustling activity to no more than a dot on some leather parchment map.

The trapper stood and walked to the prow, where Batiatus appeared by his side. "Home and dry, little man," he said, and Batiatus nodded, his head shaking faintly, the tears brimming in his bulging eyes.

. . . To be continued